No Ordinary Fortune

Judy Duarte

—

Special thanks and acknowledgment to Judy Duarte
for her contribution to The Fortunes of Texas:
The Rulebreakers continuity.

Recycling programs
for this product may
not exist in your area.

ISBN-13: 978-1-335-46554-2

No Ordinary Fortune

Copyright © 2018 by Harlequin Books S.A.

Printed in U.S.A.

www.Harlequin.com

Since 2002, *USA TODAY* bestselling author **Judy Duarte** has written over forty books for Harlequin Special Edition, earned two RITA® Award nominations, won two Maggie Awards and received a National Readers' Choice Award. When she's not cooped up in her writing cave, she enjoys traveling with her husband and spending quality time with her grandchildren. You can learn more about Judy and her books on her website, judyduarte.com, or at Facebook.com/judyduartenovelist.

To my personal hero, who always has my back, even when I'm spinning around like an ice-skater going for the gold. Sal, I love and appreciate you more than you will ever know.

Chapter One

Schuyler Fortunado had always been a family rebel, and she felt more like one today, as she drove her sporty red BMW down the highway, the back seat loaded down as if she planned to live out of her car for the next several weeks.

Granted, she hadn't actually packed the dry cleaning that hung from the rear passenger window or the bag of groceries she'd left on the back seat. She'd planned to drop them off at her condo back in Houston before starting out on her latest adventure earlier today. But she'd been so intent upon solving a family mystery that she'd hit the freeway and hadn't looked back until she'd stopped in the Texas community of Columbus for gas. The clothing would stay in the back seat, but she'd tossed out the almond milk and smoked Gouda that would go bad without refrigeration. Then, armed with a Venti coffee, she'd taken off again.

She glanced at the clock on the dash. It was late afternoon, and the traffic had slowed to an annoying rate. When her cell phone rang, she again looked at the dash, where her father's name was displayed on the screen. Kenneth Fortunado didn't take time out of his busy day for small talk, so she assumed he'd gotten wind of her latest escapade and wanted to voice his disapproval.

She was tempted to turn up the volume on the radio and let the call roll over to voice mail, but she answered instead. "Hey, Dad. What's up?"

"I didn't call to chat, Schuyler. What in the hell are you up to this time?"

"Not much. Just taking a little road trip and listening to some oldies."

He paused for several beats, no doubt reminded that she favored the same music her grandmother used to listen to, along with everything else they'd had in common.

"Where *are* you?" he asked, and not very nicely.

"I'm on a Fortune hunt."

"Oh, for Pete's sake. I told you to let that go."

"Yes, I know. But I can't ignore the fact that our family is related to the Fortunes."

"That's not a *fact*, Schuyler. You have no idea who my biological father was, and quite frankly, I could not care less."

He'd already made that clear, but Schuyler was determined to uncover the truth. And, contrary to what her father might think, she was nearly 99 percent certain that his mother's married lover had been Julius Fortune. It had been an easy conclusion to reach. The dear, eccentric woman Schuyler had called Glammy, thanks to a childhood speech impediment, had all but spelled it out during the many chats they'd had before her death.

"Daddy," Schuyler said, "I can't believe you're not the least bit interested in meeting your birth father. Or at least getting to know some of your biological relatives."

"Forget killing the damned cat, your curiosity is going to be the death of *me*—and before I get a chance to retire and enjoy life. Can't you focus on something else? Like going back to that art school or taking another acting class? You could even write that style and fashion blog you told me about."

"It's a vlog, Daddy. Besides, I can hardly concentrate on any of that when I'm so close to solving the family mystery once and for all. And don't blame this on mere curiosity. This isn't a personal quest. I'm doing it as a tribute to Glammy."

He blew out a ragged sigh that mimicked a grumble. "I suppose it shouldn't be surprising that one of my six children would turn out to be so much like my mother."

He said that as if it was a bad thing, although Schuyler wouldn't take offense. Glammy had been a little too flamboyant and over the top for the successful, straitlaced real estate mogul, but Kenneth had loved his mom. "I'll take that as a compliment, Daddy."

Out came yet another sigh over the line, this one softer and more controlled than the last. "I didn't mean that badly, Schuyler. It's just that I'm not a free spirit like my mother was. Or like you are. So I can't relate."

Both Glammy and Schuyler had embarrassed the poor man on several occasions, although never intentionally. But life wasn't meant to be boring. Nor were people supposed to be left in the dark about their past. "I'd think you'd be interested in meeting your blood kin."

"Even if your assumptions are correct, and I'm not saying they are, you do realize there was a confidentiality agreement in effect."

"I didn't sign anything."

"Dammit, Schuyler. Your grandmother did, and that's good enough for me. You need to let sleeping dogs lie—or you just might end up getting bit in the butt when you least expect it."

"Aha," she said triumphantly. "Sounds like an admission to me."

"I'm not going to admit or confirm squat."

"Maybe not, but I'd bet my trust fund that your father was Julius Fortune."

"Speaking of that trust fund, you're welcome to get a real job and join us at Fortunado Real Estate."

Schuyler could almost see him wince while making that offer, although she knew it was sincere and that he'd do whatever it took to make room for her in the family business. But they both knew that she'd never be a good fit, so she would make it easy on him, as well as herself. "I'm really not into office or corporate jobs, so that would never work."

Her father didn't immediately respond, which was just as well. They'd gone round and round on just what it was that Schuyler might actually be "into." As a result, he'd created a healthy trust account for her, just as he'd done for Glammy. He'd also threatened to cut Schuyler off on occasion, like the time she'd told him she wanted to move to Italy. He'd assumed she'd wanted to find herself, but it was more than that. She'd gravitated toward her college roommate's parents, who'd owned a villa there.

There was good reason for that. Calista's family not only welcomed her as a guest in their home, they accepted her and appreciated her uniqueness.

Schuyler wished she could say the same for her own parents. It grated on her to be the only Fortunado who was never taken seriously—and just because she danced to the beat of a different satellite radio network.

She might pretend as if it didn't bother her, but at times, disappointment rose up and smacked her in the face, taunting her with the fact that she wasn't like the others in her family. Yet how could she even try to compete with any of them? One of her brothers was a doctor, for goodness' sake. And her older sister was so determined to move up the company ladder that she'd become a workaholic.

None of that mattered, though. Schuyler wanted more out of life than that. Only trouble was, she wasn't quite sure just what "more" was. But she'd figure it out one of these days. It was just a matter of time.

A heavy silence strained the line. Finally, Daddy said, "Please don't embarrass me or the family."

Schuyler rolled her eyes. It seemed that her family shouldn't be so quick to be embarrassed. "Believe it or not, I've never set out to do that on purpose. And I'll be extra careful this time."

"I know, Schuyler. But…"

Again with the silence. Then his intercom beeped in the background.

"Listen, honey. I've been waiting for this call, so I have to go." As usual, Schuyler was saved by the corporate world in which her brilliant, business-minded father had made millions, all without the help of the Fortune family coffers he might have tapped into—had he been born on the right side of the blanket. "Just remember what I said."

"Got it, Dad. Don't embarrass myself or the family."

The call ended without a goodbye.

Schuyler turned up the volume on the radio dial, just in time to catch the beginning of the Beatles song "Can't Buy Me Love." She belted out the lyrics she knew by heart and continued her drive, wishing there was some way she could convince her well-meaning father that he didn't need to use money to keep her in step—or to buy her affection. He already had it free and clear.

She didn't particularly like being so different from everyone else in the family. Deep inside she feared that she'd never live up to their expectations, so as a teenager, she learned to embrace her inner maverick.

And that's what she was doing now. As she peered out the bug-splattered windshield, she hoped she didn't hit any more traffic in Austin. If she continued at this pace, she'd reach the Mendoza Winery offices before they closed.

If truth be told, she was nearly as eager to meet the

Mendozas as she was the Fortunes. There'd been quite a few marriages between the two clans. And from what she'd learned, Alejandro Mendoza, the owner of the winery, had a lot of handsome, single cousins. If Schuyler played her cards right, she'd be able to charm one of them into providing her with the info and the intros she needed.

Besides, it wasn't a total fact-finding mission. She'd heard their business was expanding, and she'd like to get a closer look at the inner workings of their company. At least, that's the excuse she'd give them for showing up today.

That wasn't too big of a stretch. If what she'd heard was true, their stock was going to soar in value. So she might be interested in making a personal investment.

The Houston society papers had pegged her as a ditzy trust fund baby, no matter how many charities she spearheaded. But they were wrong. And she had an impressive financial portfolio to prove it.

Either way, she hadn't set herself up for a difficult role. She was a people person, and she'd also taken several improv classes at the local junior college. So how hard could it be to win over the Mendozas and then move on to the Fortunes?

Despite the cool afternoon breeze, Carlo Mendoza had worked up a pretty good sweat as he unloaded the company truck and lugged cases of wine into the family's distribution center at Austin Commons.

Six months ago, his cousin Alejandro had asked him if he'd be willing to relocate to Austin, become the Mendoza Winery vice president and take charge of refurbishing the small, on-site restaurant.

Most of Carlo's friends had expected him to decline the offer and stay put. At thirty-five, he'd made a name for himself in Miami, working in the food-and-beverage industry. He'd managed several floundering restaurants and, in a short period, had turned them all around. He'd done the same thing with a run-down nightclub, which was now one of the most popular beachfront nightspots in Florida. But he'd jumped at the chance to become a part of the growing family organization in Texas.

Within hours of entering city limits, he'd gone right to work, planning the expansion and remodel of the eatery, overseeing the demolition and reconstruction, creating the perfect ambience and then hiring a talented chef who came up with an impressive menu.

Carlo usually preferred to stick close to the winery, as well as La Viña, the name they'd chosen for the new restaurant. But Alejandro was in the process of expanding the family business by opening a retail shop in Austin Commons. Plans were also under way for a new wine bar and a nightclub, both of which would be located on a popular downtown street. So that meant they all had to pull together.

Carlo had no more than stacked another case of wine on the cart he would wheel inside when Esteban, his father, stepped out of the distribution center. "Is that the last of it?"

"Not quite. I still need to unload the chardonnay."

After that, he would head for The Gardens at the nearby Monarch Hotel, where he'd scheduled an important tasting this evening for a group of chefs and restaurant owners attending a big culinary conference. This was the Mendoza Winery's chance to get its best vintages in the right hands, and Carlo had gone all out when setting it up. There'd be tiny white lights adorning the trees, exotic flowers on linen-draped tables and an impressive variety of gourmet cheese, crackers and hors d'oeuvres.

When Carlo had first come up with the idea of hosting carefully planned tastings, his cousin had given his hearty approval and said, "That's your baby. Run with it."

So Carlo had done just that. And up until an hour ago, things had gone exceptionally well. Then the model they'd hired to pour wine for the tasting called and said she was sick. As soon as the line disconnected, he'd immediately contacted the agency and asked them to send over a replacement. There was a lot riding on tonight's event. If things went as planned, it would launch the winery into the big leagues.

Carlo could, of course, serve the wine himself, but he'd rather be free to schmooze with attendees and lock down the sales he expected.

He glanced at his wristwatch, a TAG Heuer Carrera he'd purchased last summer, and swore under his breath. It was getting late, and the agency had yet to call back or to send another hostess. They'd told him they'd try their best to find someone. Hopefully, they wouldn't let him down.

When a car engine sounded, he glanced over his shoulder to see a red late-model BMW approaching. After parking in front of the office, next to the truck Carlo was unloading, the driver, a petite blonde, climbed out, shut the door and locked the car. When she spotted him watching her, she flashed a pretty smile.

The sight of her face alone was enough to set a bachelor's blood on fire. Add that to a pair of black skinny jeans that hugged her feminine curves and a colorful, gypsy-style top that suggested she had a playful side, and it took all Carlo's restraint not to let out a tacky wolf whistle.

She gave a little wave, as if they'd met before, then closed the distance between them with the grace and assurance of a woman who knew she had the power to knock a man off his feet. She also bore a remarkable resemblance to singer Carrie Underwood, which was merely an observation on Carlo's part. He didn't give a damn if she could carry a tune in a bucket. As long as she could pour wine, she'd work out just fine.

He'd run in the upper circles of Miami society long enough to recognize the black Chanel purse and the snazzy red Beamer, both of which announced that she lived the good life. Or that she hoped to one of these days and was trying her best to fake it until she did. He supposed that also meant she wouldn't come cheap, but at this point, he didn't care. He was desperate.

"Thank God you're here," he said. "I'm Carlo Mendoza, the one who placed the call to the temp agency. You're just in time. Let me show you what we need you to do."

She pulled up short, her expression sobered and her brow creased ever so slightly. Then her pretty smile returned and she reached out to shake his hand. "Schuyler Fortunado, at your service."

Not much took Schuyler by surprise, but when the handsome Latin hottie set aside the box he'd been carrying and swept toward her, she didn't much care what project he had in mind for her to do. She was up to the task, especially since he bore the correct last name—*Mendoza*.

He also had the perfect looks. He was tall, with dark hair that curled at the collar and expressive brown eyes. A killer smile revealed white teeth against a tanned complexion. He was definitely what she'd call eye candy. If she were a casting director, she'd sign him in a New York minute to star as the romantic lead in a major production.

She had only one question. How did he fit into the family hierarchy?

Black slacks and a white button-down shirt—crisply pressed, rolled up at the sleeves and open at the collar—announced that he was in upper management. Yet a light sheen of sweat from his labor suggested he wasn't afraid of hard work.

He reached out to shake her hand. The moment his fingers touched hers, an electrical current shimmied up her arm, giving her heart a jolt that made her pulse go wacky. She wasn't sure if he'd felt it, but she was having one heck of a time keeping her mind on the reason she was here and on the cover story she'd concocted.

"I'm glad the temp agency was able to get ahold of

you," he said. "And that you were available to help out this evening. You're a lifesaver."

Okay, so he clearly thought she was someone else. Did she dare correct him? Or should she let the mix-up play out?

"Have you ever poured wine at a tasting before?" he asked.

"No, I haven't." How hard could it be? "But don't worry about my lack of experience. I'm a fast learner."

"Consider this more of a cocktail party, only the drink options are various vintages from the Mendoza Winery. We have a lot of important and influential people attending, and your job will be to make our wines look good."

Schuyler was no stranger to parties or the nightlife. Why not play along and assume the temporary gig? It would be a fun way to get her foot in the door with the Mendozas.

"This particular tasting will be held at the Monarch Hotel," Carlo added. "It rained for the last several days, but the weather is on our side today, so we're going to have it outdoors in the garden."

"Sounds like a perfect venue." Schuyler wasn't the least bit familiar with Austin, so she didn't have a clue where that might be or what to expect from the outdoor setting, but she pasted on a big no-worries, I've-got-this smile.

He scanned the length of her from the top of her head to her strappy black heels and back again. "You look great, but I'll have to get you something else to wear."

"What'd you have in mind?" She slapped her hands

on her hips, shifted slightly to the right and taunted him with a playful grin. "A French maid's costume?"

His brow furrowed, which only lent a serious but more gorgeous air about him. "No, I meant something classy. There's a women's clothing shop just down the street. I'm sure they're still open, so we can stop there."

A smile tugged at her lips. Who would have guessed that it might come in handy to have those clothes from the dry cleaners still hanging in the back seat of her car?

"Actually," she said, "you're in luck. I happen to have an outfit with me. That is, if a black cocktail dress will work."

"That's great. Now just one last question. Do you have any experience with wine?"

"Other than drinking my share of it?" She laughed.

When he frowned, clearly not finding any humor in her response, she added, "I'm no connoisseur, but I'm not a novice, either. I know the difference between a cabernet sauvignon and a merlot. And while I don't have a wine cellar, I do keep several nice bottles at home. Also, my old college roommate's family owns an Italian villa that's surrounded by vineyards, and I spent a couple of summers there."

Finally, his expression softened, and he smiled. "You're going to work out perfectly."

Schuyler thought so, too. That is, as long as the temp agency didn't get in the way by sending someone else and blowing her chance to prove herself as the lifesaver he'd claimed she was.

Feeling a bit heroic, she strode to her BMW with a spring in her step. After unlocking the passenger door, she reached for the cocktail dress protected in plastic and hanging from the hook above the rear passenger window. She'd no more than clicked the lock button on the remote when she heard someone clear his throat.

She turned to see who it was, only to spot a silver fox and four dark-haired men, all handsome as heck and standing in an office doorway. She assumed they were related to Carlo, since they all clearly bore a family resemblance.

The older man standing front and center grinned and asked, "Aren't you going to introduce us to the lady, *mijo*?"

"Sorry," Carlo said. "Dad, this is Schuyler Fortunado, the model the temp agency sent as a replacement. She's going to be our hostess this evening."

The dashing older man offered a flirtatious grin. "I'm Esteban Mendoza, Ms. Fortunado, the father of this tribe." Then he introduced the younger men as Mark, Rodrigo, Chaz and Stefan.

Each of the Mendoza brothers was attractive in his own right. That is, if you liked the tall, dark and handsome type. Even Esteban had a debonair, heart-strumming appeal.

The DNA gods had been good to this family, and Schuyler was in her glory. Just look at the collection of hunks she'd stumbled upon. If she had to choose, she'd say that Carlo was the pick of the bunch. Either way, she'd never met a male—young or old—she couldn't charm. She was definitely going to enjoy her investigative work.

"Now that you've met my family," Carlo said, "let's

check out the setting for tonight's event. It's a short walk to the Monarch Hotel, where we've set up the tasting. Come with me."

That wasn't going to be a problem. Schuyler would gladly follow the Latin hottie anywhere.

Chapter Two

Just twenty minutes ago, the sun had disappeared into a kaleidoscope of color on the western horizon. All the while, Carlo stood next to a magnolia tree adorned with white lights and watched this evening's tasting unfold the way he'd planned it.

Several waiters, supplied by the hotel, carried trays of appetizers and moved about the garden, offering the smiling chefs and restaurant owners a variety of crackers, gourmet cheeses and hors d'oeuvres specially prepared to enhance the taste of the vintages being served. But it was the lovely blonde hostess pouring wine and entertaining the culinary experts with both her charm and wit who'd captured Carlo's full attention.

He must have caught hers, too, because every now and again, Schuyler looked across the garden, her blue eyes sparkling, and offered him a confident smile. Then she returned to her work.

She was a born hostess, it seemed, and he thanked his lucky stars the other woman had had to cancel tonight.

Just look at her. She rocked that curve-hugging dress she'd had hanging in her car. It was sexy, but not overly revealing. Classy, but still within the right man's reach.

But it was more than her outfit and pretty face that he found appealing. She had a natural effervescence, a confident demeanor, as well as an uptown style. And as a result, she'd done a good job of convincing the attendees that they should stock up on the best wines they'd ever tasted.

Schuyler flashed the label of a bottle of Mendoza zinfandel at the people gathered at her table, then poured them each a generous taste. Soft jazz played in the background, but it didn't drown out the sound of approaching footsteps.

Carlo glanced over his shoulder and spotted his father moving toward him.

"Looks like another successful tasting," the older man said.

"You're right. We've had several significant orders already. And once this group goes back to their fine-dining establishments, word about our wines will spread."

"And what about Schuyler? How's our temporary hostess working out?"

"A lot better than the last woman the temp agency sent us." She was prettier, too, which was why Carlo had been studying her with more than just business on his mind. He liked a woman with a playful side, especially since that usually meant she wouldn't expect a long-term commitment.

Carlo had already experienced a failed marriage and wasn't about to make that mistake again. He was too much like his father, he supposed.

"I'm proud of you, *mijo*. You put a lot of work into this evening, and it shows."

"Thanks." Carlo had never lacked confidence, at least not in the business world. Still, his father's praise meant a lot. "I've always gone above and beyond to pull off a successful event, but it's even sweeter when that success benefits the family."

"Sounds like you're settling in here."

Carlo stole a quick glance at his father, but he didn't see a need to respond.

"Are you happy you came to Austin?" Esteban asked.

"So far, so good. Why?"

"Don't get me wrong, *mijo*. But you have to admit, in the past, you sometimes got bored with a job after a while and moved on to what you'd called bigger and better things."

Carlo would like to object, to tell his father that he'd always had good reason to make a job change from one restaurant or nightclub to another, but some of what he said was true. Sometimes boredom had played a role. "Don't worry, Dad. That's not going to happen this time."

"I'm glad to hear that."

The two men continued to watch the tasting, as well as the pretty blonde hostess.

"You had a lot of friends in Miami," his father said. "And a busy social life. I worried that you'd miss all of that."

"Not really, although I'll admit it's been a bit of an adjustment." It had been six months since Carlo had turned over the keys to his ocean-view apartment and drove to Austin. Yet his enthusiasm for both La Viña and Mendoza Winery was stronger than ever. "I'm still in contact with some of my friends and making new ones. Besides, this position is a good fit, especially since I'm working with family."

"It's been a good change for me, too. So was re-uniting with my brother. That took a huge weight from my heart."

"I know." Carlo, as well as his brothers, had noticed the positive changes in their father ever since he and Orlando had buried the hatchet. After a decades-old riff, everyone had been shocked to learn that Esteban had actually fathered Orlando's son, Joaquin Mendoza. The man Carlo thought was his cousin was actually his half brother. Recently, Orlando and Esteban had forgiven one another for the past, and Esteban was now getting to know Joaquin as his son.

"You're watching Schuyler with a keen eye," his father said. "Are you waiting to see if our temporary hostess makes a mistake? Or are you planning to follow up this tasting with a romantic evening?"

"She's not going to screw up. Look at her. She's in her element."

Esteban chuckled and slapped a hand on Carlo's shoulder. "Apparently, she's caught your eye, *mijo*. And something tells me you don't plan to thank her for a job well done and then send her on her way."

"Let's see how the rest of the night unfolds." Carlo glanced at his watch. Things would be winding down soon. The chefs and restaurant owners would be heading to dinner, and that left him and Schuyler to debrief following the tasting.

He knew better than to mention that plan. Of all Esteban's sons, Carlo was the most like their father, a dynamic, charismatic guy who had an eye for pretty women—and a bit of trouble with commitment. Yet none of that seemed to matter. Neither of them had ever had a shortage of dates.

"Schuyler keeps glancing this way," his father said. "So I'd venture to say that she's got her eye on you, too."

It seemed that way. And she wasn't looking at him like an insecure employee hoping to get her boss's reassurance. No, Carlo could spot sexual interest in her eyes.

In a few minutes, he'd ask her to celebrate the successful tasting by joining him at dinner. And something about that playful gleam in her pretty blue eyes told him she wouldn't turn him down.

Schuyler was having the time of her life. The garden setting was perfect, the evening festive. She'd never sold wine before, but she knew how to talk to people. And she'd soon found those in attendance, all men and women in the culinary industry, to be worldly and interesting. By the end of the tasting, she'd snagged several large-scale orders for the winery, and she'd had a fabulous time in the process.

As the chefs and restaurant owners filed out of the garden and the hotel cleanup crew moved in, Carlo made his way to the linen-draped table where she'd been stationed for the past hour or so.

"You were amazing," he said. "I couldn't have asked for a better hostess."

"Thanks for the vote of confidence. I never realized that work could be as fun as a cocktail party."

"I suspect you've attended your share of those."

She answered with a flirtatious grin, which he lobbed right back at her. From what she'd seen so far, all of the Mendoza brothers were gorgeous, but she had to admit that Carlo was by far the most attractive—and appealing. She couldn't pinpoint one single reason for making that conclusion. Actually, there were several—his drop-dead good looks, the playful intensity in his gaze, his confident air. On top of that, she also respected the way he'd orchestrated tonight's event then stood back and watched it all unfold the way he'd planned.

There was clearly more to him than met the eye. There was something under the surface that also sparked her interest, a sexy yet teasing style that gave her reason to believe he might be as interested in having fun as she was.

Some people shouldn't expect a romance to last forever, Glammy had said, *and I'm one of them. Why compromise my dreams and values just to be accepted? Doing that will only lead to failure, disappointment or heartbreak.*

Schuyler had to agree with her grandmother's philosophy. As the middle Fortunado daughter, she was used to coming up short in her parents' eyes more often than not.

Admittedly, she wished her father would be proud of her—just the way she was. Not that she'd suffered any lack of confidence because of his disappointment over the years. After all, she'd honed an innate ability to change direction whenever she needed to, something she considered a valuable asset, especially when there were a lot of miserable people in this world who'd do better if they followed their hearts.

"I can't begin to thank you for stepping up at a moment's notice," Carlo said. "You really knocked it out of the park tonight. Would you be interested in pouring wine at our future tastings?"

"Sure. Why not?" Talk about getting her foot in the door with the Mendoza family. Now she wouldn't have to mention anything about a possible investment, although the idea intrigued her.

Carlo tossed her a heart-strumming smile. "That's great. Let's celebrate a job well done."

"Good idea." Schuyler didn't always experience the joy of accomplishment, but she did tonight. Was this how her sister Maddie felt whenever she closed a big deal? She shook off the thought and asked, "Would it be okay if I tried some of the Red River merlot? I told everyone it was my favorite Mendoza wine, even though I'd never had your label. I wouldn't want my nose to grow and sprout leaves."

"Like Pinocchio, huh?" Carlo chuckled as he reached for two clean glasses and set them on the table.

"Exactly. I loved that story, especially the cartoon.

Besides, I have a thing about being honest." While that was basically true, a niggle of guilt rose up inside, reminding her that she'd neglected to admit that she wasn't the woman he thought she was.

Had he been impressed enough with the job she'd done that she could tell him about the mix-up? Would he get angry? Or would he laugh and let her hang around him and his family for a while?

She'd called Nathan Fortune yesterday as a follow-up to a letter she'd sent him last week. But before making a five-hour drive to visit him in person, she wanted to get a better feel for the renowned Fortune family. Who knew what the Mendozas might reveal or what questions she might have after talking to them.

Carlo pulled the loosened cork from one of the half-full bottles and made a generous pour. Then he handed a glass to Schuyler.

She thanked him and took a sip, savoring the hint of black cherry. No wonder some of the chefs had raved about it. "This is very good."

"I'm glad you like it." He held up his glass to the outdoor light overhead, flicked his wrist ever so slightly and watched the wine swirl. Then he returned his attention to her. "So how'd you like working this event tonight?"

"I had more fun than any of the attendees." And standing outside under a canopy of twinkly lights adorning tree branches with a handsome Latino made it all the better.

It was, however, getting a little chilly. She took another sip of merlot, hoping it would warm her from the inside out. Yet she still gave a little shiver.

"You're cold," he said.

"Just a little. It's not bad enough to run back to my car for a sweater."

"I'm not sure if I told you that's a pretty dress. It was perfect for the tasting tonight."

"I have plenty more like this one at home."

"I'd be disappointed to learn that you didn't. I assume that means you like to go out on the town."

"Every chance I get." She offered him another spunky grin, noting his playful expression. Apparently, he was enjoying her company as much as she enjoyed his.

"You've got to be hungry," he said. "I certainly am. Why don't you join me for dinner?"

"I'd like that. Just give me a chance to freshen up. I'll use the hotel restroom."

Ten minutes later, after running a brush through her hair and reapplying her lipstick, Schuyler stopped by the registration desk in the front lobby. She needed a place to stay while she was in Austin, and the Monarch was certainly convenient.

After checking in for the night and getting a key, she returned to the garden, which was now empty—thanks to the efficiency of the hotel cleanup crew.

"Ready to go?" Carlo asked.

"Yes. Are we walking or driving?"

"If you're okay with Italian food, we can walk. There's a great little restaurant a few blocks from here."

"I love all things Italian." And Latin, it seemed.

"Then let's go. It's close to the office, so you can get a sweater or jacket from your car, if you want to. Either way, it's a short walk."

When he offered her his arm, she took it, hoping to absorb some of his body heat. "Lead the way."

Carlo blessed her with a dazzling grin that could turn a girl's knees to mush. Then he guided her along the sidewalk to the street.

Her heels and the soles of his loafers tapped a steady beat, and while she should probably remove her hand from his forearm, she enjoyed his warmth, as well as the taunting scent of a masculine soap that complemented his sea-breezy cologne.

"How long have you worked for the temp agency?" he asked.

Uh-oh. She hadn't minded playing along with the identity mix-up at first, but she wasn't ready to reveal her hand quite yet. What if he had some kind of commitment with the agency that he thought had sent Schuyler as a substitute hostess this evening? What if he reneged on the job offer to hostess future tastings?

She'd have to face that possibility, but maybe it would be best to tell him over dinner—or even dessert.

"Would you believe this was my first time on the job?" she asked.

Okay, while that wasn't an out-and-out lie, it wasn't completely honest. But still, it was somewhat truthful. She'd never been a hostess for a wine tasting before.

"Well, you'd never know it from my vantage point. You were a champ."

Moments later, they approached Rossi's, a small

brick building with a black wrought iron railing that provided an enclosure for curbside dining. Several portable heaters supplied warmth for a few couples who'd taken a seat outdoors.

"Inside or out?" Carlo asked.

"It doesn't really matter to me."

"Then let's take the first available table." He opened the green door for her, just like a gallant Latin lover, and she entered the small restaurant that boasted white plastered walls and dark wood beams.

The place had an old-world charm, right down to a colorful mural on the east wall and a rustic fountain in the back. And if the aroma of tomatoes, basil and garlic was any clue, the food had to be good.

"Two for dinner," Carlo told the hostess.

"This way." The hostess reached for two leather-bound menus, then led them to a linen-draped table, which was adorned with a red rose in a budvase and several flickering votives.

Carlo pulled out Schuyler's chair, and she took a seat. Then he sat across from her.

The hostess handed them the menus. "Your waiter is Alfonso. He'll be with you in a moment."

Moments later, a short balding gentleman in his fifties stopped by their table, introduced himself and took their drink order.

"We'll have a bottle of Mendoza merlot," Carlo told Alfonso.

"Nice choice, sir."

Schuyler couldn't help but smile. "Did you choose

this place because of the food they serve—or because of their wine selection?"

He leaned forward and said, "The food is excellent. And for that reason, we offered a tasting here a couple weeks ago. The customer reaction was so positive that the owner placed an order. So I'd also like to be supportive."

Schuyler set her menu aside. "So tell me. What's it like working for a family business?"

"It's pretty cool. We all get along—and we have a common goal. We want to see the winery be the best it can be."

"That's nice." Schuyler supposed Maddie felt the same way about Fortunado Real Estate.

Carlo studied her for a moment, and a slow smile stretched across his gorgeous face. "You've got pretty eyes."

"So do you," she said. "Some women would trade just about anything for long, thick lashes like yours. I hadn't noticed until I saw them from this angle—and in the candlelight."

"Thank you. As a kid, my brothers used to tease me about them."

Siblings could sometimes be cruel without meaning to. "I'll bet that made you feel bad."

"No, it made me double up my fists and let them have it."

She laughed. "I'll bet it did. So did you guys fight a lot growing up? I'd imagine, with all that testosterone flowing, there'd be some pretty big power struggles."

"Sometimes, but it was usually just in fun."

When Alfonso returned with their wine, they grew silent, waiting for him to uncork the bottle and pour them each a glass. Then, after telling them he'd be back with water and to take their order, he left them alone.

They'd hardly taken two sips when Carlo's phone rang. He glanced at the display, then said, "I don't normally take calls at the dinner table, but this one might be for you."

Schuyler arched a brow. What made him say that? Who knew she was here—other than his father and brothers?

"Yes," Carlo said. "Speaking."

His brow furrowed as he pressed the phone closer to his ear. "Oh, yeah? No, that's not a problem. At least, not yet. Can we talk about this tomorrow?" After a moment, he nodded. "Thanks."

Schuyler leaned forward, wondering if he'd tell her who'd called—and why he thought they'd want to speak to her. She'd never been especially patient.

"That was the temp agency we've been working with," he said. "They were apologizing because they couldn't find a fill-in for the hostess who canceled out on us."

Uh-oh. Schuyler bit down on her bottom lip. Too bad she hadn't been up-front with him when she'd first arrived. Or given him her cover story about wanting to make an investment. He probably would have accepted her help anyway. And she would have saved herself from an awkward moment.

His eyes narrowed as he speared her with an assessing look. "So who are you?"

* * *

Schuyler's eyes widened, and her lips parted. Apparently, Carlo wasn't the only one who'd been thrown off stride by that phone call from the temp agency.

He leaned forward, his arms braced on the table, and waited for her answer, which she seemed to be pondering. That wasn't a good sign.

Several beats later, she brightened. "You know…" She lifted her index finger and gave it a little twirl in the air between them. "It's funny you should ask."

"I don't find it funny. Why did you lie to me?"

"Whoa, now just wait one minute. The only thing that was the least bit dishonest was the fact that I never set you straight when you assumed I was the woman sent by the agency. But other than that, I was up-front with you. My name is Schuyler Fortunado, I know a little about wine and I spent two summers at a friend's Italian villa."

At this point, he questioned everything about her.

"All right," he said. "Then assuming that's true, why'd you let me believe the temp agency had sent you?"

"I can be a little impulsive at times, and I like to have a good time. Serving wine at a classy event sounded like fun. Besides, it was pretty obvious that you needed my help."

He didn't doubt any of that, especially the part about his needing her help. And while he was still suspicious, he had to admit that she fascinated him. Why not enjoy his time with her this evening, even if only to discredit her?

"Okay, I can buy the fact that you had fun tonight. You're also a natural at serving wine and schmoozing. What kind of work do you do?" Modeling immediately came to his mind. Acting, too. And if that were the case, she had to be pretty successful at it. That car she drove and the purse she carried weren't cheap.

"Actually, I'm currently unemployed."

He wondered why. She'd admitted to being impulsive. Had she walked off her last job? Had she been fired? Temporarily laid off? And what position had she held up until that time?

Rather than pepper her with those questions, he asked, "How do you pay the bills?"

At that, her smile faded. "You're about to learn that I'm honest, even if it's not something I care to admit."

Oh, wow. Was she a high-end call girl? If so, he hadn't seen that coming.

"My father set up a trust fund for me," she said, "so I really don't have to work. But that doesn't mean I'm not looking for the right job."

A trust fund baby, huh? Daddy's little girl, too.

"Are you an only child?" he asked.

She laughed. "Sometimes I wish that I were, even though we're all fairly close. I have three brothers and two sisters."

"And they're all supported by trust funds?"

"No, just me."

Carlo lifted his glass and took a slow, steady sip. The woman was as interesting as she was gorgeous. He was usually pretty good at pegging people, but he wasn't having much luck with her tonight.

"My brother Everett is a doctor," she added, "and my sister Maddie works for my father's real estate company. But I'm more of a free spirit who dabbles in the arts, so my dad feels compelled to take care of me, like he did my grandmother."

Carlo wasn't used to women being that open and up-front—assuming that Schuyler was being forthright now.

She fingered the stem of her wineglass, then looked up and caught his eyes. Her beauty alone was staggering, but the sincerity in her gaze nearly stole his breath away. "Just so you know, I'm not always going to be on the family dole. I've gone to college and traveled abroad. I just haven't quite figured out what I want to do with my life, and at twenty-five, I don't think that's too unusual."

"No, I don't suppose it is. I went through a time in my life when I was unsure about what I wanted to do." At twenty-five, after his divorce, he'd been forced to reevaluate his future, and that had left him a little out of step for a while.

"Apparently," she said, her blue eyes glimmering, "you've got your life all sorted out now."

"In time, it all came together." He studied her in the candlelight, the lush blond locks, the heart-shaped face. Some men could lose their heads over a woman like her. That is, if they didn't drown in those sparkling blue eyes first.

But Carlo wasn't about to let his hormones run away with him. "I'm glad you came along when you did, but that doesn't explain why you happened to be at the distribution center in the first place."

She lifted her wineglass and took a sip. "I'd heard some interesting things about the winery and wanted to check it out for myself. I might even want to purchase some stock."

He supposed that was possible, and while he wanted to believe her, he was still a bit skeptical.

"So tell me," Schuyler said, "have you lived in Austin all your life?"

"No, I'm originally from Miami. I moved here six months ago."

"And you're working for your cousin now." It wasn't a question. The lady must have done her homework. But he supposed that wasn't so hard to figure out.

"Your family must be pretty close," she added.

They hadn't always been, but things were looking up between his brothers and his cousins. "I guess you could say that."

"Is your side of the family as close to the Fortunes as some of the other Mendozas are?"

Now there was a question that didn't sit right. Something about it was...off.

"Okay," he said. "What are you really up to?"

"Nothing," she said.

Yeah, right. "You can't play a player, Schuyler. Whatever scheme you're cooking up, I've probably already attempted it myself."

She blinked, and her lips parted. For a moment, he found himself softening. But he didn't dare let down his guard. "Listen, I can't be bought, sold or conned.

But there's one thing that might persuade me to open up and answer your questions."

"What's that?" she asked as if she seriously wanted to know what might tempt him.

"The truth."

Chapter Three

Schuyler hadn't meant to be deceitful. Nor had she tried to "con a con man." So it really ought to bother her to have Carlo assume that she was playing him. But in reality, she was a bit turned on by the fact that he wasn't like other men—and that she couldn't charm him into submission, like she was often able to do.

As Carlo continued to stare at her as if reading her innermost thoughts, as if he understood her better than anyone else in the world, she realized, for some inexplicable reason, that she actually wanted him to.

"Who *are* you?" he asked again, his demeanor cool and unaffected.

Admiration and attraction went up another notch. "I told you before. My name is Schuyler Fortunado, but you can also call me Schuyler Fortune."

He furrowed his brow, clearly confused—and unconvinced.

She'd better explain. "Gerald Robinson's father is my grandfather—which makes Gerald my uncle. But my father was illegitimate and kept secret from the family."

"But why'd you show up here, at the Mendoza Distribution Center?"

"Because I want to get to know the Fortunes. Rather than pop in on them unannounced, I decided it would be best to take a slow-and-easy approach in meeting them. And since the Mendozas have strong family ties with them, I thought I'd start with you."

"I'm not going to be very helpful."

"Maybe. Maybe not. Either way, you have to admit that today turned out to be a win-win for both of us. You needed my help. And I needed to meet someone who knows the Fortunes, even if it's by six degrees of separation."

"You also need a job." Carlo sat back in his seat, no doubt stretching out his legs under the table. "Money, too, I suspect."

So he didn't believe what she'd told him about the trust fund and thought she was in it for a payday. That's where he was wrong.

Schuyler lifted her wineglass and took another sip. "Contrary to what you might think, the Fortunes' wealth has nothing to do with this. You see, just like my uncle, Jerome Fortune, aka Gerald Robinson, my father is a self-made man."

"So you say." The intensity of his gaze nearly bored into the very heart of her, but he was way off.

"Why are you so skeptical of me?" she asked.

"Shouldn't I be?"

"I suppose it's only natural." She blew a little sigh out the side of her mouth. He wasn't going to be an easy man to win over. And oddly enough, that made him all the more appealing.

"Just to be clear," he said, "the Fortunes are experts at recognizing impostors and gold diggers."

"No doubt they are, but I can assure you, some people don't need a famous name to be successful. If you're smart and the cards are in your favor, you can make it to the top. And my father is as smart as they come. He's lucky, too. A real King Midas. He parlayed a winning lottery ticket into real estate, and his investments paid off. He now lives in the most exclusive area of Houston and owns an agency in a downtown high-rise, with branches in Austin and San Antonio."

"Fortunado Real Estate?"

"That's us. So, you see, we don't need the Fortunes' money."

Before Carlo could answer, Alfonso stopped by the table with a basket of bread, olive oil and balsamic. Then he took their orders.

When they were alone again, Carlo picked up the conversation where they'd left off. "If your family has plenty of money, why the interest in the Fortunes?"

"Actually, my father and most of my siblings aren't interested in forging a connection. At least, that's what they told me." She reached into the basket, removed a warm slice of bread and tore off one side of the crust.

"I suspect they're curious, but they're not sure about making any changes to our family dynamics."

"And you're not concerned about that?"

Schuyler wouldn't mind seeing a slight shift in the Fortunado family dynamics. For one thing, she'd like to see artistic expression valued as much as an advanced degree or a head for business.

"I'm more open-minded than the other Fortunados," she said. "So I decided to check out the Fortunes for myself."

Carlo studied her once again, as if he still couldn't buy her story. She lifted her wineglass and took a drink. Dang, it was good. No wonder those chefs had been impressed.

"Believe it or not," Schuyler said, "I'm as honest as the day is long."

"Except when you hold back information."

"Well, that's true." She popped the crust into her mouth. Mmm. Homemade and fresh from the oven.

"It seems to me," Carlo said, "that you'd be better off talking to Ariana Lamonte, who wrote those articles and blogs for *Weird Life* magazine about the Fortunes."

"I already did." Apparently, he didn't realize she'd done her homework. "Her articles actually convinced me that my suspicion was right and triggered my quest. And by the way, in case you didn't know, her last name is Fortune now. She married Jayden Fortune from Paseo, Texas."

"So your visit to the Mendoza Winery Distribution Center was plan B?"

"I hope that doesn't hurt your feelings."

At that, he laughed. "I'm just on the periphery of the Fortune family, but I can get you an introduction if you'd like one."

"That's great. And I promise that I'll watch from the outside. I don't mean them any harm. Think of me as an investigative reporter."

"And a damn pretty one at that."

Now, that was an interesting way to toss out a compliment. But then again, with the way he looked and his sexy style, it was easy to see Carlo had plenty of practice—no doubt from a string of sexual conquests over the years.

"Ariana can probably provide you with a better introduction to the Fortune family than I can," Carlo said.

"You're right. And once she and her hubby get back home in a few weeks, I plan to talk to her about doing that."

He scrunched his brow, creating a crease in his forehead, but it didn't mar his gorgeous face in the least. "Where are they?"

"They're out of town while she researches a new book about people who embody the Texas spirit."

Before Carlo could respond, his cell phone rang again. He glanced at the screen. "Believe it or not, I'm not usually a rude dinner companion, but I need to take this call. If you'll excuse me, I'll step outside and answer it. But I'll make it quick."

She nodded. Like Daddy had taught her since she was old enough to join the family at the dining room table, business always came first.

Once, when Schuyler was in high school, a friend

called her while they were having dinner. Her father threatened to take away her cell phone if she answered. Yet two minutes later, he got a call and took it. When he finished talking, she pointed out the inconsistency, which made him angry. He lifted his finger and shook it at her. *Here's the rule in this family, Schuyler. When a phone call earns money, you answer it.*

Moments later, Carlo returned to the table. He'd no more than taken a seat when he leaned forward and zeroed in on her like a con man who'd found his mark. "I have a proposition for you. I need your help again, and I'll do whatever you want if you agree."

Schuyler raised her eyebrows. "Whatever I want? Just what would this job entail?"

"Now who's being skeptical?" Carlo laughed. "There isn't anything unsavory about it. I need someone to represent the Mendoza brand at another special tasting. You just have to do the same thing you did this evening. Pour wine and get people to drink it—and hopefully buy it. I'll pay you well for your time."

"I told you before. This isn't about the money. I don't have to work a day in my life unless I want to."

And if truth be told, she wanted to hostess again for Carlo.

"So what do you say?" he asked.

She was always up for an adventure. So she reached across the table to shake his hand and seal the deal. "It'll be a pleasure doing business with you."

In spite of his better judgment, Carlo had been listening to Schuyler half in amusement, half in curiosity.

But things got serious the moment he took her hand and felt the unexpected strength of her small grip, the softness of her skin and the heat of her touch. Desire slammed into him, nearly taking him out at the knees.

He tried to play it cool, to hide his sexual attraction, but he'd never met a woman like her before. And he probably never would again.

Granted, he'd been skeptical of her the moment he'd learned the temp agency hadn't sent her and she'd let him believe that they had. In some ways, he supposed he was still a bit leery, but she seemed sincere.

She was also gorgeous and as intriguing as hell. Besides, she was the best hostess they'd had yet. And she was damn good for business. Bottom line? He was going to take a gamble and believe her story.

"The next tasting is on Thursday evening," he said. "Are you available to work that night?"

"Three days from now?" She tucked a strand of hair behind her ear, revealing a good-size diamond stud. "Sure. I'll be in town for a while."

She didn't say how long she intended to stay, and even though he was growing more and more curious about her plans, he didn't ask. "Thanks for being flexible," he said.

"Hey. That's practically my middle name." She flashed him a dazzling smile, then leaned forward. "So tell me about this 'special' tasting."

"There's going to be another convention in town. This one is for a group of software execs. So I called the people in charge and set up a special preconference event. We negotiated a discounted price, and they liked the idea."

"Is it going to be in the Monarch Hotel gardens?"

"No, this one will be held at the winery. We're sending a bus to provide them with transportation to and from the hotel. Then, after they have a tasting of our best vintages, we'll serve them dinner."

"Sounds like an exciting evening for a group I'd expect to be a little dull and boring in real life."

Carlo laughed. "Leave it to a party girl to make that assumption."

She gave a little shrug, followed by a playful wink.

"Actually," he said, "a lot of thought goes behind my invitation for a special tasting. Those executives all live in various parts of the country, so I figure they'll order several cases each and share it with their friends when they get home. It's a good way to get the wine into the hands of consumers outside Texas."

"I like the way you think."

"Hey, when you have a good product or business, the best promotion is word of mouth."

"Looks like you've thought of everything."

"I try to." He leaned back in his chair and lifted his glass. Yet he found his dinner companion more tempting than his favorite Mendoza wine.

Damn, she was pretty. Carlo prided himself on his strength and character, but God help a weak man who found himself attracted to her.

"Is your tasting room open daily—or just by special request?"

"We're open in the afternoons, and we have a host

who handles the regular tastings for us. He also works at La Viña in the evenings, so I'd prefer to use someone else during our special events."

"So that's where I come in."

"Exactly. And as part of your pay, I'll do whatever I can to help you be that fly on the wall with the Fortunes."

"I'd really appreciate that." Her eyes were an interesting and unusual shade of blue. They also were assessing him just as carefully as he'd studied her moments ago.

"I'm not blowing smoke," he said. "There's going to be a Valentine's Day party at the Mendoza Winery on the fourteenth, and a lot of the Fortunes will be there. You can be the hostess that night and 'work' the room."

Her smile practically lit the entire restaurant, extinguishing the need for the votives on the table. "That would be great, Carlo. You won't be sorry. I'll be professional and discreet."

He hoped she was right, and that his belief in her hadn't been unfounded. After reaching into the pocket of his sports jacket, he pulled out his business card and handed it to her. "In the meantime, why don't you stop by the winery tomorrow morning. I'll give you a personal tour."

"I'd like that."

Interestingly enough, Carlo would, too.

Bright and early the next day, while Schuyler was sound asleep in her suite at the Monarch Hotel, the alarm went off.

Normally, she hated wake-up calls or sticking to a

schedule. But not this morning. Without a grumble or even a yawn, she threw off the covers, rolled out of bed and padded to the bathroom.

She stopped long enough to glance in the mirror, expecting to see her hair a sleep-tousled mess, but it didn't look all that bad. That in itself was a surprise, but even more so was the smile that stretched across her face. She'd always had a natural effervescence, but it didn't usually begin to surface until after her first cup of coffee. But then again, today was different. Her wish was about to come true. In less than two weeks, she was going to be face-to-face with some of the Fortunes.

How cool was that?

Yet there was something else giving her reason to celebrate. She was going to see Carlo again.

Dinner last night had not only been delicious and filling, it had been…well, interesting—to say the least. It had also bordered on romantic.

As a rule, she steered clear of men who might want a serious relationship with her. She didn't need any more people trying to pressure her into conforming to their expectations. But she suspected that Carlo was different.

For that reason, before turning in last night, she'd set the alarm on her smartphone to give her plenty of time to get ready.

An hour later she was driving out to the winery and following the directions Carlo had given her. After turning into the driveway, she couldn't help easing her foot from the accelerator and slowing down to take in the acres of grapevines growing in the Hill Country.

Another storm had passed through during the night, drenching the area in rain. But after watering the plants and flora, as well as cleansing the air and leaves, it had passed through and the sky was now clear and blue.

It was certainly pretty here in the country. Schuyler had always been a city girl, but that didn't mean she didn't enjoy breathing in fresh air and watching the sun set over rolling hills and greenery. Not that she'd be invited to stay at the winery that long, although she'd be up for extending her visit.

She'd no more than parked and shut off the ignition when Carlo came out to meet her. If she'd thought he looked handsome last night, he was even more striking today in khaki slacks and a white cotton shirt—button-down, crisply pressed. Definitely not a Texas cowboy. More like a tall, dark Miami Beach hottie.

"Welcome to the Mendoza Winery," he said.

She left her purse, a big black Chanel she'd filled to the brim with various items she might need at any given moment, and locked the doors. Then she placed the keys in the front pocket of her jeans and greeted him with a handshake. The formality wasn't necessary, but she wanted to touch him again, and a hug didn't seem appropriate. Maybe she'd offer him one when she left.

"What do you think of the place so far?" he asked.

"It's impressive. You'd never know that your cousin bought it recently. It's been so well cared for that you'd think your family has owned it for years."

"It was in the Daily family for generations, and Alejandro purchased it from them."

"Either way, the grounds are beautiful."

"Thanks. It's been a team effort. Actually, it still is. We're going to expand more so we can offer it as a venue for parties and weddings. Come on. I'll give you that tour, starting with the sculpture garden around the back."

Schuyler fell into step beside Carlo. In addition to taking in the lovely grounds, she couldn't help breathing in his alluring, ocean-fresh scent and losing focus. As they turned the corner and she spotted the sculpture garden, she realized why he thought the setting would be perfect for weddings or special events.

"This is amazing." She scanned the rose garden, and the manicured lawn that had been adorned with several large sculptures.

"We're going to plant more flowers," he said. "And we've ordered a Spanish-tiled fountain, which a local artisan is going to create. The stone sculptures were already here—and permanent. But we're going to bring in other outdoor art pieces and rotate them."

"That ought to be a nice touch." She stopped to admire the statue of a cavalry officer mounted on a horse. "This is pretty cool."

"I think so, too."

She circled to the front of the horse and placed her hand on its nose, stroking it as if the animal was real. Then she looked at Carlo and grinned.

"Come on. I'll show you the tasting room next." He placed his hand on the small of her back. Her spine tingled at his touch, an electrifying flash that shot through her like a sparkler on the Fourth of July. Her legs wobbled, and she nearly stumbled before making a quick recovery.

If Carlo noticed, he didn't comment. Instead, they crossed the garden, returned to the back of the main building and entered. Just down the hall, a sign on a large, rough-hewn wooden door announced the tasting room hours. He gripped the brass handle and opened it for her, then he followed her inside.

She scanned the open reception area, which boasted high, vaulted ceilings and dark beams, as he led her to a marble-topped bar. Shelves of corked wine bottles awaited the next batch of wine enthusiasts who would come to taste the best vintages the winery had to offer.

"Has your family always been in the wine business?" she asked.

"No. When Alejandro was in college, he got a part-time job working at a South Beach wine bar to put himself through school. And that's where it all started. He changed his major to agricultural operations and went on to get a master's degree in viticulture and enology. He also spent a summer in France interning at a vineyard and another summer in one located in Napa Valley."

"I can see where his interest took off from there. I told you about my friend Calista, whose family owned that villa in Italy. It wasn't quite the same for me, but her enthusiasm was almost contagious, and I learned a lot during my visits. For a while, I thought about moving there, but my dad had a fit and threatened to cut me off for good." She turned and studied Carlo. "But what about you? What made you leave Miami to work at a winery?"

"I come from a long line of restaurant and nightclub owners, so I've got a solid handle on the food industry, as well as wine. One of my jobs with Mendoza Winery is to run La Viña."

"Are you the manager?" she asked.

"I suppose you could say that. Alejandro let me have free rein in remodeling the restaurant and hiring a chef and waitstaff."

"I'd love to see what you've done."

"We'll end the tour there, then have lunch. In the meantime, I'll show you the vineyard and the cellar, where we make the wine."

Carlo led her outside and to a barn, where a red electric car awaited them.

"Oh my gosh," Schuyler said. "How cute is this? It looks like a cross between a golf cart and a limousine."

"It's new," Carlo said. "And another of my suggestions. I thought it might be a nice touch for small, intimate tours. And Alejandro liked the idea."

So did Schuyler. "You've got a great business sense. I'm impressed."

"Thanks." Carlo glanced at her, his brow slightly scrunched.

"What? You don't believe me?"

"No, it's not that."

"Then what's wrong? And don't tell me *nothing*. Doubt is splashed all over your face."

He slowly shook his head and smiled. "It's not doubt. It's surprise."

"Don't tell me that you don't realize how bright and creative you are."

His mouth tilted in a crooked grin. "Actually, I've never had a problem with self-confidence. I just hadn't…" He paused, clearly trying to choose his words carefully. "Well, I didn't think you'd look at the business side of things."

Her brow shot up, and she folded her arms across her chest. "You didn't think that a trust fund dolly could spot a potentially lucrative operation or notice someone with a clear head for business?"

"I didn't mean to question your intelligence. It's just that some women would be oohing and aahing about the winery and more impressed by the family's successful new venture."

"You mean your family's financial status?" Schuyler rolled her eyes and clicked her tongue. "You've definitely been dating the wrong women."

Carlo laughed. "I'm not sure about that, but I can tell you this—you're not like any of them."

She brightened. "You know what? I'm going to take that as a compliment."

"You should." He swept out his arm toward the classy golf cart in an after-you fashion. So she climbed into the front seat and waited for him to join her.

Moments later, he started the engine and took off to show her the property, stopping several times to point out different vintages of grapes.

Despite the sun, there was a bit of a chill in the air, especially as they zipped along the narrow blacktop road just big enough for the cart, but Schuyler wasn't about to complain. Not when she was getting a private tour of a beautiful Hill Country vineyard by a handsome Latino.

When she'd mentioned the women he dated, which had been his cue to reveal whether he was committed to anyone in particular, he hadn't even blinked. She could probably come right out and ask, but she didn't want him to think she was interested in him.

Okay, so she was. More than a little—and more than she cared to admit.

Carlo probably had his contact list filled with the names and numbers of beautiful women, each of them eager to have his attention. Schuyler would bet her trust fund that he wasn't the kind of guy who spent many Saturday nights alone.

She didn't, either. Not that her dating life was all that active. She preferred to keep things light, fun and unencumbered. And that meant that she almost always came home alone. It was easier that way.

But maybe she ought to reconsider her philosophy on men and dating. She wouldn't mind going out on the town with Carlo Mendoza on a Saturday night—or any night of the week for that matter.

They turned to the left, onto a small dirt path that was still damp from the recent rain, dodging several puddles along the way.

Schuyler didn't like taking vehicles off the road. When she was fifteen, Glammy took her out to practice driving her classic Volkswagen, a hot pink Bug Glammy called Mary Kay.

Since you don't have a learner's permit yet, Glammy had said, *your father will freak if I take you on the pub-*

lic highway. Let's go out in the country. I know just the place.

It had been raining earlier that day, and when they got out onto the dirt road, they'd soon sunk axle deep. So much for Glammy's good intentions. Daddy had freaked anyway, especially when he got the towing bill.

"Aren't you afraid of getting stuck?" Schuyler asked Carlo.

"No, I drove out here with Alejandro yesterday, before he left for a seminar in California. And we didn't have any trouble getting through."

The vineyards continued to stretch along the right shoulder, but when Schuyler's gaze turned to the open hillside on the left, she gasped and pointed. "Look at those bluebonnets. I'd heard they were going to bloom early this year. Would you mind pulling over so I can get a picture?"

"Not at all." Carlo stopped along the side of the pathway and waited while she pulled her smartphone from her pocket and headed off to get a good shot.

Schuyler might have dropped out of art school, but that didn't mean she didn't appreciate natural beauty. And sometimes, she liked to dabble in watercolors. If the painted version of that hillside turned out as good as she hoped it would, she'd frame it and hang it in her bedroom at home.

She caught movement to the right and spotted a longhorn cow lumbering toward a rusted-out farm tractor. Now there was an unusual sight. She raised her cell phone, snapping a picture first, followed by a video.

How cool was that? As she backed up, continuing to

film what she suspected was a stray cow, she stepped in a puddle that practically swallowed up her Jimmy Choo ankle boot and knocked her off balance. Before she could blink, she plopped to the ground, splattering muddy water.

"Dang it," she muttered, as she glanced at her drenched leather boot, hoping it was waterproof and not ruined. Sheesh. She'd had the pair for only a few months.

Before she could get to her feet, Carlo was at her side. "Are you okay?"

"Just a little dirty and wet. But it's no big deal."

He reached out his hand, and she took it, allowing him to pull her to her feet.

"I'll take you back to the winery so you can clean up," he said.

"That's not necessary. A little mud never hurt anyone, but that puddle did a real number on my Jimmy Choos." She brushed her dirty hands together, then wiped her palms against her denim-clad hips and smiled. "Oh, well."

His eye twitched, and one side of his lips quirked into a crooked grin. "You're something else."

She wasn't sure what he meant by that, but a humorous spark in his eyes indicated he hadn't meant it as a criticism.

"In what way?" she asked.

"Most women would be flipping out about the dirty water and mud, not to mention the ruined boot."

"I told you that I'm not like most women."

"You were right." He studied her face for a moment,

his gaze locking on hers. Then he lifted his hand and brushed the pad of his thumb against her cheek.

"Did the mud splatter up that high?"

"Just a little." His cleaning efforts turned soft, gentle, tantalizing. Surely her face hadn't gotten that dirty.

She could have stepped back and taken over wiping her cheek of a lingering smudge, but she liked his soul-stirring touch. His eyes seemed to be caressing her face, too, setting off a quiver in her belly.

"Did you know that the color of those wildflowers is the same shade as your eyes?" he asked.

Her breath caught. "No, I didn't."

"They're pretty."

"The bluebonnets?"

"Your eyes."

About the time she thought he might kiss her, he nodded toward the cart. "Let's head back to the winery so you can dry off and clean up before you catch cold."

She didn't much care about the mud or the wet foot or the chill in the air, but she headed back to the cutesy little cart like a soggy damsel who'd been rescued by a handsome prince.

"I can't believe you're not concerned about ruining that shoe."

"It's not that I don't care. But whining about it isn't going to help."

Besides, their budding friendship or whatever was sparking between them just might prove to be a lot more valuable than a pair of pricey shoes.

Chapter Four

"Do you have a change of clothes?" Carlo asked Schuyler on the way back to the winery.

"I keep a packed gym bag in my car, which always has yoga pants, a shirt and shoes."

"Good." He drove the cart to the parking lot, pulled alongside her BMW and waited until she removed a black canvas tote from the trunk. Then he took her to the entrance of La Viña and parked in front. "There's a restroom inside. After you clean up, we can have an early lunch."

Once they climbed the steps and reached the double glass doors, Carlo pulled out his keys while Schuyler studied the hours posted on the sign.

"The restaurant doesn't open until five o'clock," she said.

"That's right. We offer a brunch on weekends, but we

only serve dinner on weekdays. That's going to change in the future. Word has already spread about our menu and the service, so we've been seeing an increase in the number of diners."

"So you were right," she said. "Word of mouth is the best promotion of all."

"Ah, you were listening."

"Always." Her eyes sparkled with mirth. Or flirtation. It was hard to tell. "But I'm a little confused. If the restaurant is closed, how are we going to have lunch?"

"Don't worry." He tossed her a smile. "I don't need a chef to put out a nice meal. Go change your clothes. I'll wait for you here, then we'll raid the fridge."

"That sounds like fun, not to mention clandestine." She winked, then disappeared into the bathroom.

Women, especially the pretty ones, tended to take a lot of time fussing with their appearance, so Carlo expected a long wait. But when Schuyler returned just moments later wearing a lime-green tank top, black yoga pants and gray running shoes, he was again reminded that she wasn't anything like his usual dates.

She'd run a brush through her hair and applied pink lip gloss. He couldn't help noting that she rocked that stylish, curve-hugging outfit. The good Lord had blessed her with a great shape, and it seemed that she worked hard to keep it that way.

Apparently, she hadn't noticed his admiring gaze, because she scanned the restaurant interior, her blue eyes wide, her lips parted. "This is amazing."

She was amazing. But she was talking about the renovation he'd designed. She pointed to the large windows that provided an unrestricted view of the vineyard, as well as the rounded oak-paneled ceiling that resembled the shape of a wine barrel. "I'm impressed. This would be the perfect venue for a wedding reception."

"You'd consider getting married here?"

At that, she balked. "Who, me? Oh, no." She slowly shook her head, those luscious blond locks tumbling along her shoulders. "I'm too much like my grandmother to consider making a lifelong promise like that."

"Your grandmother never married?"

"No. At one time, she'd actually hoped Julius Fortune would follow through with his divorce, which he'd told her was in the works, although it really wasn't. I can't believe that lothario was able to juggle so many affairs without his wife catching him."

"Who says she didn't know? I'll bet some people would put up with just about anything for money."

Schuyler blew out a *humph*. "Not me."

He believed her. She wore wealth and status well, but he figured she didn't consider money to be a cure-all. Neither did he, which meant they might make a perfect match, one that wasn't encumbered by well-intentioned vows most people found hard to keep.

"Come on," he said. "I promised you lunch, although it's going to be a joint effort."

"I'd be happy to help, but will the chef be upset to find out that we're taking over his kitchen? I'd suspect that he'd be a little territorial."

"I do this all the time, so he won't mind."

Once in the kitchen, Carlo pulled out the fixings for

a garden salad, along with some grilled chicken and a small container of dressing left over from last night.

"What can I do to help?" she asked.

"Why don't you fix a fruit and cheese platter? I'll make a salad."

While they worked, Carlo put a small loaf of French bread in the oven to warm.

"Where'd you learn your way around a kitchen?" Schuyler asked.

"I've worked in restaurants for years and learned a few tricks from several of the chefs. How about you? Do you like to cook?"

"Not especially. But then again, it's not too much fun preparing food for one. So I eat most of my meals out." She reached for a bunch of grapes, rinsed them and placed them on the cheese platter, alternating clumps of green and red. Next, she added apple slices.

"Good job," he said.

"Thanks." She glanced at the bowl he'd filled with a spring mix of greens, tomatoes, mushrooms, avocado, pine nuts and chopped chicken. "That looks good, too. I'm impressed."

He gave a slight shrug. There didn't seem to be any reason to tell her that most of the women he dated liked having him cook for them. He'd have them sit on one of his kitchen bar stools and pour them a glass of wine. Then, while soft jazz played in the background, he'd fix one of his special dishes, like chicken marsala. It was part of the foreplay.

Yet this was different.

Or was it?

He kept his thoughts to himself as he and Schuyler set the food out on a table in the dining room, next to a window that looked out on the sculpture garden. He held out her chair, and after she took a seat, he sat across from her.

"That cheese platter looks great," he said.

"I have an eye for color and design. Or so I've been told."

"Did you ever think about doing something with that?"

"Actually, I went to art school for a while, although I dropped out—something that upset my dad." Schuyler plucked a green seedless grape from the cluster on the cheese board and popped it into her mouth. "He couldn't understand that my time there wasn't a waste."

He found himself leaning forward, intrigued. Maybe even entranced. "I'm sure you benefited from your time there. Why did you find it valuable?"

"I learned a lot and I definitely have an eye for color and design, but I really haven't put any of it to good use—as my dad reminds me sometimes."

"So you're a colorful, fun-loving tumbleweed for the time being."

Her smile dimpled her cheek. "I guess so. But I have another focus right now. And that's to sort through the family mystery, although it's not the least bit mysterious to me."

"The Fortune connection."

"Exactly." She reached for a rice cracker. "In fact, I'm going to take a drive out to Paseo tomorrow and visit Nathan Fortune."

"That's one long-ass drive for a little chat."

"I figure Paseo is about five hours from here. If I leave early in the morning, I should be back by late afternoon or the evening."

Carlo nodded, as if it all made sense to him—this quest to meet her family. "So why Nathan? How does he fit into all of this?"

"He's pretty much an outsider, so he probably has an interesting take on the dynamics. When I read his sister-in-law's articles in *Weird Life* magazine, I remembered some of the things Glammy told me about my dad's biological father, and I connected the dots."

"Glammy?"

"Sorry." She smiled and placed a small slice of white cheddar on her cracker. "I was trying to call her Grammy, like the other kids in the family, but I had a speech impediment when I was a little girl, so that's how it came out. And the nickname stuck. Anyway, Glammy and I were very close."

"She sounds like an interesting character."

"She's gone now, but Glammy was pretty unique, and I idolized her. On the other hand, her unique personality sometimes embarrassed my dad."

"In what way?"

"Well, for example, I went to a private high school in an exclusive part of town. On the night I graduated, she showed up wearing a tie-dyed T-shirt and a pair of fluffy bunny slippers. I thought a vein on my dad's forehead was going to burst."

"Did it embarrass you?"

"No, not at all. Glammy showed me how to tie-dye

one summer, and we had fun making matching tops. So that was her way of letting me know she remembered the fun we'd had that day, which was pretty special. And the slippers? I'd given them to her for Christmas. Besides, she'd had an ingrown toenail, and she chose comfort over style."

"You must have loved her a lot."

"I really did. You have no idea how much I miss her. We were a lot alike. Two orange peas in a purple pod, my dad used to say."

"Does that mean you own a pair of bunny slippers?"

She laughed. "I wish I did, but no. My dad wasn't too happy that my grandmother and I had so many similarities. For example, she had a penchant for art, mostly retro stuff, psychedelic colors and that sort of thing. She was the first one to encourage me to express myself artistically. And she stepped in and convinced my dad that it wasn't a bad thing for me to transfer from college to an art school. He'd just about gotten used to the idea, when I decided to come home after two semesters. He doesn't let me forget that I sometimes disappoint him, like she used to."

"Tell me more about your grandmother."

Schuyler brightened. "She was amazing. Years ago, when she lived in San Francisco, her name was Mary Johnson. She was working at a nightclub and met Julius. That's when he told her he was in the process of getting a divorce. They hit it off, and he put her up in a fancy Houston condominium. She'd assumed that he would eventually be free to marry her, but Julius wasn't interested in making an honest woman out of any of his lovers."

Carlo poured them each a glass of iced tea. "When did they break up?"

"When Glammy got pregnant with my father, it was the beginning of the end. Julius asked her to sign a confidentiality agreement, promising to give her the deed to her home and to leave her financially comfortable. He also insisted that she name their son Kenneth rather than one of her unconventional suggestions. She agreed, and the affair ended."

"Did she admit to you that Julius was your grandfather?"

"Not in so many words. She honored that confidentiality agreement, although keeping that secret just about killed her. When my dad was six, she legally changed their last name to Fortunado. I think she chose a Latin form of the name she believed we all deserved but could never claim. She also changed her first name to Starlight, which my dad never understood."

"Starlight? Sounds like a hippie name."

"Yes, but you have to remember she lived in San Francisco in the 1960s. And just between us, I think the name suited her a lot better than Mary did." Schuyler used her fork to spear a piece of chicken from her salad. Before popping it into her mouth, she added, "My dad loved his mother, even though he considered her to be a little too flamboyant and over the top. I'm sure that's why he chose a quieter life for himself."

"And you didn't?"

"Life wasn't meant to be boring. And just so you know, Glammy wasn't a flake. She was one of a kind."

"It's easy to see that you admired her."

"And adored her. She loved all of her grandchildren, but there was a special place in her heart for me. Over the years, we became especially close, and when she died, I was heartbroken. I was also determined to live my own life the way Glammy had."

"And that means being a little out of step with the other members in your family."

"Yes, but that doesn't bother me. Although I must admit, that's one reason I'd like to ease into the Fortune family. I'd like to get to know them before they have a chance to judge me."

"I can't imagine them finding you lacking in any way. And I'm surprised your father doesn't appreciate you for being unique."

"That's nice of you to say." She paused, as if pondering whether she should share more or not. "I'm happy with things the way they are. But to be completely honest, when my younger sister, Valene, started working for Fortunado Real Estate, it stung a bit."

"Why is that?"

Her response stalled again. "I'd never be happy working in an office, but it's a little disappointing to be bypassed in the hierarchy of the family business, especially by my younger sister."

"I'm sorry."

"Thanks, but I'd never be a good fit anyway."

"So here you are," he said, "doing your own thing and searching for your family roots."

"Pretty much. I'm also doing it for Glammy. She always dreamed that her son and grandchildren would be recognized as Fortunes, and that's my dream now. Hopefully, they'll end up being the kind of people I wouldn't mind knowing or claiming as family."

"I guess there's only one way to find out. You'll just have to meet them." He reached for a cluster of purple seedless grapes and pulled off a couple. "Are you going to keep your room at the Monarch Hotel?"

"Yes, of course. I have a nice room there, so why pack up and look for someplace else to stay?"

"So you're not planning to get a room in Paseo tomorrow night?"

"I'm going to leave early in the morning and will head back in the afternoon. I'm determined to make the trip to Paseo and back in one day. From what I can see from the map, there's not much between here and there."

"I'll be in town again tomorrow," he said. "Maybe I can buy you a drink when you get back to Austin. Then you can tell me how your visit with Nathan went."

"That's sounds fun. We can be partners in crime."

"I don't know about that, but something tells me it might be a lot of fun getting into trouble with you."

"Now there's an intriguing idea."

Wasn't that the truth?

Carlo was eager to see Schuyler again, for drinks and a debriefing.

An evening couldn't be more intriguing than that.

Schuyler peered out the bug-splattered windshield. Her GPS indicated she was getting close to her destination. And from the looks of the small town up ahead, she was. That is, if the meager set of single-story buildings that hadn't seen any new construction since FDR's New Deal was Paseo, Texas.

Talk about being down in the boondocks. She'd driven hours to get here, and within a blink or two, she'd be leaving the town in the dust. Even though she hadn't seen a car in ages, she hit her turn signal and turned off the highway, following the directions she'd been given.

Nathan Fortune knew she was coming. She'd mailed him a letter to begin with, asking him to please call her. When they'd talked on the phone, he'd been pretty quiet. But she hoped to draw more out of him when she met him in person.

"Hi there," she said, practicing her announcement aloud, "I'm your long-lost cousin."

No, that wasn't true. You couldn't lose a relative you didn't know existed. And none of the Fortunes, legitimate or otherwise, realized they were related to the Fortunados—a soon-to-be-revealed secret.

Her family had always teased her about being too impulsive, about following her heart rather than her mind. But how could she do otherwise? She often got a gut feeling about things and couldn't let it go until she saw it through. Besides, she seemed to have a killer instinct for knowing when something felt right. And, like it or not, meeting her Fortune relatives felt better than right. So when her father had told her to back off on her quest, she hadn't been able to.

It wasn't like she planned to waltz right up to the

upper echelon of the family hierarchy and blatantly introduce herself.

She scanned the countryside. Wow. Talk about living outside the inner circle. Nathan must be a hermit. Of course, living way out here, in the middle of nowhere, he'd almost have to be.

When she spotted a line of bent and rusted-out mailboxes along the side of the road, she muttered, "There it is." Then she followed the graveled drive to a two-story house.

She'd no more than parked near the big barn and gotten out of the car when she was met by a shaggy brown-and-black dog with a red-and-white Western bandanna tied around its neck. It barked several times to announce her visit.

Then again, maybe it was in warning. For a moment, she wondered if she should climb back in the safety of her BMW, but the mutt really didn't look all that mean or vicious.

"Hey," she said, "don't worry about me, doggie. I'm friendly. Gosh, I'm actually family."

The dog seemed to understand and trotted up to her, giving her a curious sniff. Moments later, a man walked out of the barn, all big and buff and cowboy.

"Hi there," she called out, as she reached across the dog to greet him. "You must be Nathan. I'm Schuyler Fortunado. But you probably already gathered that."

"Yep. I figured as much."

She scanned her rustic surroundings, which were also clean and neat. "I don't expect you get too many visitors way out here."

"You've got that right." He gripped her hand and gave it a sturdy shake. "But I kind of like it that way."

She supposed he'd have to. "You have no idea how happy I am to meet you. Thanks for agreeing to see me."

After releasing her hand, he lifted his hat and wiped the sheen from his forehead with his sleeve. "I can't imagine why you'd come all the way out here to talk to me. It's a long drive just to say hello. You must have something on your mind."

Schuyler might be a little impulsive, but she was as honest as the day was long. "First of all, like I mentioned in my letter, I've been on a hunt for my family roots, and I finally solved the mystery when I read your sister-in-law's articles in *Weird Life*."

His brow creased, but he didn't respond.

"Don't get me wrong, Ariana is a great writer and investigative reporter, but she came up short in uncovering all the Fortunes out there. There are more of us than she could've imagined."

Nathan continued to stare at her, his unspoken questions deepening the furrow in his brow.

"Your father didn't corner the market on infidelity," she said. "Julius Fortune was as big a tomcat as his son was."

Nathan adjusted his hat on his head, then folded his arms across his broad chest. "What are you getting at?"

"I'll cut to the chase and hit the high points. Years ago, Julius had an affair with Mary Johnson, my grandmother. While she was pregnant with my dad, they split up."

"I've never heard of a Mary Johnson, and I've read Ariana's columns."

"Well, that's probably because she legally changed her and my father's last name to Fortunado. She was always partial to things with a Latin flair. Or any kind of flair, really."

Nathan continued to gaze at her as if he didn't know what to make of her. Or her story.

"So why'd you come to see me?" he asked. "Why not go all the way to the top with your claim?"

"Because I'd like to observe the family for a while."

The front door squeaked open, and an attractive brunette in her late twenties stepped onto the porch. She lifted her left hand to shield her eyes from the midday sun, revealing a diamond ring, and made her way to Nathan.

His expression softened, and his eyes brightened at the sight of her. "Bianca, this is Schuyler Fortunado, another one of my cousins, it seems."

Bianca had to be his wife, the woman he'd recently married. She crossed the yard, her long straight hair sluicing down her back, and greeted Schuyler with a smile. "It's nice to meet you."

Was it? Schuyler had pretty much just dropped a bombshell. At least, that's how she'd feel if the tables had been reversed and Nathan had shown up at her condo in Houston and made a similar announcement.

"I'm sure you didn't expect to hear that there are more of us," Schuyler said.

Nathan and Bianca looked at each other, as if weighing how to respond.

"Well, actually…" Nathan began, "we're not all that surprised."

Schuyler frowned. *Had* they known about her?

"Ariana spent months tracking down elusive Fortunes and was the one who'd found me and my brothers," Nathan said. "She mentioned that there was another branch of the family, but I made a point of not listening. So if you're looking for information about any of them, I'm not the person you want to talk to."

"But that's exactly why I'm here. I want an honest, unbiased opinion from someone who isn't swayed by the family's money or influence or even its drama."

"I'd be happy to give you one, but I've never met any of them, including the man who was my sperm donor."

Now it was Schuyler's turn to be surprised. "Aren't you interested in meeting Gerald Robinson—or should I say Jerome Fortune?"

"It's a little late to be looking for a daddy at my age. I'm more interested in keeping him away from my mom, Deborah. So the less contact I have with the man, the better."

That was an interesting flip. Schuyler was dying to meet them all, while Nathan wanted to avoid them. "Is something wrong with Gerald—or with the rest of the family?" That thought hadn't crossed her mind, but maybe it should have.

"Some of them are okay, I guess. Why?"

"I'd like to meet with them. Any of them."

"I can't tell you much about the Robinson branch of the family. You'll need to go to Austin for that. You can also go to Red Rock and Horseback Hollow to learn about the others, some of whom are married to Mendozas. But for the record, some of them may not be as welcoming as others. Kate Fortune has been subjected to plenty of phony gold diggers over the years."

Schuyler had, of course, heard of the family's matriarch. "I'm not the least bit interested in the family money or in Kate's cosmetics company. So she doesn't scare me."

"Then maybe you should talk to her or one of the others," Nathan said. "I'm not privy to or interested in any of the family dynamics."

Before she could remind him that she didn't want to make a big splash, the screen door creaked open, then slammed shut as a small boy dashed outside. "Mommy, can I have another cookie? I'm super hungry and I've been good all morning."

Bianca smiled. "You also picked up your Legos without me asking, so yes. But let me get it for you, okay?"

"This is our son, EJ," Nathan said, boasting a happy grin.

Schuyler couldn't help but admire the little guy. "He's darling."

"He can also be a real pistol at times," Bianca added. "But he's been exceptionally good this morning, so if you'll excuse me, I'd better get that cookie before he tries to get it himself. I'd be happy to put on a pot of coffee, if you'd like to come inside."

"Thank you," Schuyler said, "but I need to go."

As Bianca and EJ returned to the house, Nathan studied Schuyler. "So will you be heading to Austin to talk to some of the Fortune Robinsons?"

"Eventually, but rather than barge in on them, I have another connection. The Mendozas."

"Sounds like a viable option," Nathan said. "Good luck."

She thanked him for his time, then headed for her car. She had another long drive in front of her. She wanted to be back in Austin before the end of the workday.

Or to be more exact, before the cocktail hour began at the Monarch Hotel.

Chapter Five

Carlo sat in the upscale lounge of the Monarch Hotel, a red glossy gift bag resting discreetly on the floor next to his chair. Nearly an hour ago, just after four o'clock, Schuyler called to let him know she'd hit the Austin city limits and to ask where to meet him.

He figured she'd been on the road long enough, so he'd suggested the hotel where she was staying.

Now, here he sat, watching the happy hour crowd with a glass of wine in front of him. He'd ordered the Lone Star, the Mendoza Winery's prize chardonnay, from the cocktail waitress, a quiet-spoken blonde in her thirties who'd introduced herself as Patty.

He'd taken only a couple of sips when Schuyler entered the lounge with a bounce in her step and a pretty smile on her face. You'd never have known that she'd spent the last ten to twelve hours driving.

She must have gone upstairs to her room to freshen up and change into the stylish little black cocktail dress she'd worn for a couple of hours for the tasting two nights ago. She looked just as sharp this evening, just as sexy. Maybe even more so.

As she approached his table, he stood to greet her, then he pulled out a chair for her. "How'd your visit with Nathan go?"

"It went okay. He's a nice guy, and I'm glad I had the chance to meet him, his wife and their sweet little boy. But he really didn't say anything to quench my curiosity about the family."

"Did you expect him to?"

"No, not really. But at least I've met him face-to-face. And now I have an in with him and his brothers."

"You'll also have a chance to meet more of the Austin Fortunes at the Valentine's Day party," he reminded her.

"That's true."

Carlo took his seat, motioned for Patty the cocktail waitress, then asked Schuyler, "What would you like to drink?"

"What are you having? Is that the Lone Star?" When he told her it was, she said, "I'll have that, too."

Once Patty arrived at their table, Carlo ordered another chardonnay.

"I poured quite a few glasses of Lone Star at that tasting, and several people raved about it. So I'm looking forward to trying it."

"I'm glad to hear that. You can't very well sell our wines if you haven't tasted them all."

"I agree."

He studied her a moment, the way her vibrant personality shined in her eyes, the way her blond tresses tumbled over her shoulders.

"What's the matter?" she asked. "Don't tell me I have spinach in my teeth."

He laughed and slowly shook his head at her humor. "No, I don't see anything out of place."

Only trouble was, he couldn't blame her for wondering why he was gawking at her. And he'd be damned if he wanted her to think he was caught up in his attraction.

"I was just admiring that pretty dress," he said. "It looks nicer on you each time I see it."

"Thanks. But don't worry. I'm going to do a little shopping while I'm in Austin. I have a closet full of appropriate evening wear at home, but I'm not going to drive back to Houston to get them. Especially after the tiring road trip I just made."

"I'm sure you're beat after going all the way to Paseo and back, but as a side note, you don't look all that tired to me."

"Maybe not. But I'm going to turn in early tonight. I have a feeling one glass of wine is going to do me in."

He didn't know what he'd been expecting, other than having a drink or two with her tonight. Dinner afterward, maybe. And possibly a visit to her room. But she'd just set the parameters.

Patty returned with Schuyler's drink, as well as a

small silver serving dish filled with mixed nuts. After she left them alone, Carlo reached under the table for the surprise he had for her. "Since you're going to kick back and relax after that drink, I thought I should give you this."

At the sight of the red gift bag, Schuyler's eyes widened. "I don't understand. What's this?"

"It's no big deal. Just something to show my appreciation for a job well done." He hoped she didn't think it was an early Valentine's Day gift. Of course, maybe it didn't matter what she thought until she peeked inside.

So he handed her the bag, eager to see the look on her face when she opened it and saw what he'd scored while shopping earlier today.

Schuyler loved surprises. She also loved presents, no matter what the cost. Over the years, she'd learned that it was often the least expensive things that meant the most. Yet before looking inside, she studied the bag in her hands for a moment, stunned that Carlo would give her a gift. "This is so unexpected."

"Aren't you going to open it?"

"Yes, of course." She pulled out the tissue paper and gasped at the fluffy white items inside. "I don't believe this." She withdrew one bunny slipper by the ear, then the other.

"I guessed at the size. So if they don't fit, you can exchange them."

"I'm sure they're perfect." As her eyes filled with tears, she did her best to blink them away. "I don't know how to thank you. This is the best gift ever. Where'd you find them? I mean, you must have taken the day off work and scoured every store in Austin."

He tossed her a boyish grin. "I'm not about to reveal all my secrets. But I have to admit, this is the first time I've given a present to someone who really appreciated it."

"Seriously?"

"Yep. And that smile on your face means it was a great investment."

An investment? "Were they expensive?"

"So asks the multimillionaire's daughter." Carlo laughed. "Don't worry. They were running a sale on bunny slippers at Dillard's in The Domain mall."

"I find that hard to believe, but thank you for putting so much thought into this. You're something else, Carlo. I can't believe a woman hasn't snatched you up and put a ring on your finger."

"Yeah, well…I was married once, but it didn't work out. I've come to believe that I'd be better off not making serious commitments."

Musical chords sounded in the background, followed by a microphone sound check. Schuyler glanced across the room, where a long-haired musician with a guitar and another with a keyboard were setting up so they could entertain people in the bar. But she was more interested in the handsome Latino who'd proved to be both generous and thoughtful.

He'd admitted to being married before, and if he'd decided not to make that mistake again, he must have been hurt by it. "I take it your divorce was painful."

"Actually, it was more disappointing than anything.

I'd never failed at anything in my life, so it was a hard pill to swallow. But then again, my parents didn't have a good marriage, either. So you can't blame me for being realistic about people not following through on those kinds of promises."

"Tell me about her."

"Who? Cecily? What do you want to know?"

"Whatever you feel like sharing. I'm curious about the woman who stole your heart."

"I don't know about that. I mean, I thought I loved her at the time, but in retrospect it was probably just lust. In the bedroom, things were good. But outside? There were problems from the start."

"Why's that?"

"I was only twenty-four, and she was two years younger. We were both headstrong and naive, and within a year, we were divorced."

"You don't think you could have worked things out, even with counseling?"

He shrugged a single shoulder. "I doubt it. To make matters worse, Cecily wanted babies right away and I wasn't ready. Besides, I didn't think we knew each other well enough."

"Maybe you didn't ask yourselves the right questions."

"That's possible." He grew solemn for a moment, then glanced at his nearly empty wineglass. When he looked up, he slowly shook his head. "I'm not sure why I'm telling you this. I have friends—good ones back in Miami—and I never shared any of the details with them."

"I'm easy to talk to, I suppose." That was probably why Glammy had told Schuyler more details about her love affair with Julius than she'd told her other grand-children.

As one of the musicians sang the Otis Redding hit "(Sittin' On) The Dock of the Bay," Carlo reached out his hand. "Dance with me. This song reminds me of the ocean and my old stomping grounds."

He didn't have to ask her twice. She'd always loved this song. So she took his hand and let him lead her to the dance floor. He opened his arms, and she stepped into his embrace, swaying to the sultry tune.

The scent of Carlo's unique cologne reminded her of late-afternoon walks in Galveston, where she and Glammy had sometimes slipped away for what they called "girl time."

But as Schuyler rested her head against Carlo's shoul-der as they moved to the sensuous beat, she wasn't having thoughts about afternoons on the bay. She was thinking about nighttime in an Austin hotel.

But that was crazy. It was too early, too soon to have thoughts like that. And as impulsive as she could be at times, making love with a man she'd met only a couple of days ago was sure to be a mistake.

When the song ended, and Carlo released her, she nearly swooned. She blamed it on the long drive and on that glass of wine that had gone right to her head, giv-ing her romantic thoughts she didn't dare trust.

"I hope you don't mind if I call it a night," she said.

"No, I understand."

They stood on the dance floor for a moment, which

only gave her second thoughts about saying good-night. He'd said that since his divorce, he'd been avoiding serious commitments. That ought to make her feel better about having a short-term affair with him.

But for some reason, she wasn't opposed to striking up a relationship that might last a little longer. Because a man who'd gone out of his way to find her a pair of bunny slippers just might turn out to be a keeper.

She placed her hand on his chiseled jaw and placed a kiss on his cheek. "Thank you so much for the slippers."

"You're more than welcome."

That was her cue to leave, but she found herself vacillating. She was tempted to hang out for another glass of wine and one last dance. Either that or she could take him by the hand and lead him to the elevator.

She wasn't that buzzed. If and when she invited Carlo to her room, she didn't want her thoughts distorted by alcohol, lack of sleep or starry eyes.

"I'll make this up to you," she said.

"You already did."

He probably thought she meant her appreciation of his thoughtfulness and generosity, but it went beyond that.

"I'll see you on Thursday," she said. "And don't worry. I'll be there early, fully rested and prepared with my A game."

He gave her a dazzling smile that nearly stole her breath away. Then she walked back to the table and retrieved her purse and the gift bag. After taking one last glance at Carlo, she turned and headed for the elevator—alone. And wondering if she'd just made a big mistake.

* * *

True to her word, Schuyler arrived at the winery on Thursday afternoon an hour early and wearing a stylish red dress. On another woman, Carlo might have considered it a classic. But on Schuyler, it looked downright sexy. Talk about bringing her A game.

"You look great," he said. "Apparently you had a successful shopping trip yesterday."

"I certainly did." She gave a little twirl. "Will this do?"

He admired the red dress that hugged her curves. "It's perfect. Red is my new favorite color."

She laughed. "Oh yeah? What color used to be your favorite?"

"When we were at the Monarch Hotel, it was black."

"Great line, Carlo. But then again, I'm sure you've had a lot of practice charming the ladies."

True. But he hadn't been trying to charm Schuyler. That compliment was genuine and had just rolled off his tongue.

"Come on," he said. "I'll show you how we've got things set up for this event."

She fell into step beside him, and he took her inside the winery and to the tasting room, where they'd placed a sign on the large, rough-hewn wooden door that read: CLOSED FOR PRIVATE PARTY FROM 3 PM to 5 PM. PLEASE COME AGAIN.

Carlo reached for the brass handle and pulled open the door for her. Once she'd entered the reception area, he walked her to the marble-topped tasting bar, where she would be posted for the next two hours. Behind her was a tall linen-draped cocktail table holding an array of wineglasses, and a shelf with the corked bottles she would serve this afternoon.

"When it gets closer to three, the chef will send out a variety of gourmet crackers and cheeses, as well as sliced baguettes and fruit on that wooden trestle table."

"Is there anything else I need to know?" she asked.

"You certainly don't need instructions on how to be a hostess. Just do what you did the other night."

"Will do. But just so you know, I'm going to try and break my last sales record."

"Maybe I should pipe in music to set the mood. Something like 'Lady in Red' would be perfect."

"Hey. Are you trying to sell me or the wine?"

Actually, the thought of any other men ogling her and having romantic ideas didn't sit very well. But then again, he didn't have a claim on her. So he shook off the momentary jealousy and smiled. "You don't need any props, honey."

"Neither do you." If his term of endearment surprised or bothered her, she didn't let on.

He nodded toward the door. "Do you want a snack before the bus gets here?"

Her eyes sparkled with mirth. "Why? Do you want to raid the chef's fridge again?"

"No, we'll have to ask what he can spare. He's already back there, preparing for dinner."

"Cool," she said. "I'd like to meet him."

For a moment, Carlo's gut clenched. Bernardo Santos, the new chef he'd hired, was in his mid-thirties and had an eye for the ladies. Not that it mattered, he supposed. Schuyler was free to date anyone she wanted.

"Then come on. I'll introduce you." Carlo placed his hand on Schuyler's back and ushered her out of the tasting room and toward the kitchen. He could have walked next to her, his arms at his sides, but oddly enough, he didn't let go.

Instead, as their shoes clicked upon the tiled floor, he let his hand linger on her lower back as if staking his claim.

The tasting was in full swing, and the software execs seemed to be enjoying the wine Schuyler served them. She had to admit, they weren't the nerdy and boring group she'd expected them to be. Some of them were actually bright and witty.

Of course, there was usually one in every crowd that proved to be a jerk. And the guy wearing a ninja T-shirt and a black sports jacket was no exception. One of the others mentioned that Ninja Guy had been downing tequila shots at the restaurant where they'd had lunch.

With each sip of wine he took, Ninja Guy grew louder and more political. But it was impossible to decide whether he leaned to the left or right, because he voiced a loud and contrary response to any opinion.

"So how 'bout those Broncos?" he asked, switching from politics to sports. "Are you into football, pretty lady?"

"I'm not a huge fan, but I'll watch the Super Bowl on Sunday."

"I've got tickets to the company skybox," Ninja Guy

said. "Let me show you how the rich and famous watch the game."

A couple of the others at the table rolled their eyes. Schuyler was half tempted to do the same thing, but she'd promised Carlo she'd be a professional this afternoon.

In the meantime, she was cutting off Ninja Guy. He'd had way more than his share of wine, not to mention the tequila buzz he'd had when he arrived.

Carlo, who'd stepped out of the tasting room to write up several orders, returned to announce that dinner was being served in the main dining room. Those lingering in the tasting room began to file out the door. But not Ninja Guy.

He sidled up to Schuyler as she was replacing the cork in an open bottle. "Hey, sweetie. Why don't I help you clean up, then you can join me for dinner."

Carlo stiffened, but he clamped his mouth shut. She suspected he was tempted to speak up, to put the guy in his place. But he couldn't very well make a scene, especially when Ninja Guy had ordered several cases of the Lone Star, as well as the Red River. Why set him off?

"Thanks for the offer," she said, "but I've already eaten. So you go on to La Viña without me."

"Then join me in there for a drink. We can talk about watching the Super Bowl in that skybox."

"Sorry," she said. "I already have plans to watch the game with friends."

"You gotta be kidding me." He reached across the marble-topped bar and grabbed her hand.

The moment he touched her, Carlo moved across the

room, no doubt planning to come to her rescue. But he didn't know Schuyler very well. She was capable of taking care of herself.

She jerked her hand away and pointed her index finger at Ninja Guy, jabbing it at his chest. "Listen, jerk. I don't like to show off, but I've had years of karate training and have a black belt. You wouldn't want to limp back into the restaurant, sporting broken ribs, would you? I'd think that would embarrass you in front of your colleagues."

"Sheesh," he said, taking a step back. "I had no idea you were so temperamental."

Okay, so she'd lied and claimed to have a black belt, when she'd gotten only as high as green before telling her parents she was done with sports and had moved on to country line dancing.

"Mr. Layton," Carlo said. "Your friends are looking for you."

"Okay, I'm going." He nodded toward Schuyler and told Carlo, "Watch out for that one. She might be pretty, but she's got a mean streak."

As he shuffled out of the room, listing to one side, Schuyler looked at Carlo, who was shooting daggers at the drunk. His glare offered a warning that was as tough as any bouncer she'd ever watched in action.

When the door clicked shut, Carlo's expression softened. "I'm sorry about that. Usually, the people who come to our tastings are classy and don't arrive already liquored up."

"Don't worry about it. No harm, no foul."

Carlo slowly shook his head. "It took all I had not

to kick his butt all the way to the bus that brought him here."

"Maybe it'll do him good to get some food in his belly."

"Speaking of food, let's go get something to eat."

She tucked a strand of hair behind her ear, hesitant.

It's best to keep a man guessing, Glammy used to say. And in this case, maybe it was.

"Actually," she said, "I was thinking about heading back to the hotel. I'd rather not have to cross paths with Ninja Guy again. Otherwise, I might have to prove my skill at karate."

"Were you serious about being a black belt?"

"I'm afraid I was really stretching the truth. Not that I don't know some defensive moves I could have used on him."

A slow smile stretched across Carlo's face, creating boyish dimples in his cheeks.

"Just so you know," she said, "I can take care of myself. You wouldn't have had to kick his butt."

"I'll make a note of that." He nodded toward the door. "If you're dead set on heading back to the hotel, I'll walk you to your car."

"That's nice, but again, I'm not afraid of that guy."

"I didn't make the offer to protect you, although I'm definitely willing. But my mom insisted that I respect women, whether they have black belts or wear sexy red dresses."

"Aren't you a charmer."

"You say that like it's a bad thing."

"No, actually I'm a bit in awe of it." Then she reached out and slipped her arm through his. "Let's go."

As they stepped outside, the sun was setting, taking what little warmth it had provided earlier, and a crisp winter chill filled the air. Schuyler leaned into Carlo, absorbing some of his body heat and savoring his ocean-fresh scent.

She had half a notion to change her mind, to tell him she'd stick around after all. It wasn't like Glammy had been an expert on men or romance.

Did Carlo have any idea how appealing Schuyler found him? And not just as a person or a boss. But as a man. The guy was smart and personable. Generous and thoughtful, too. Who else would have thought to give her bunny slippers?

When they reached her car, she kept her arm in his, unwilling to let go yet. Apparently, he wasn't in any hurry, either, because they remained like that for a while.

"What do you have planned tomorrow?" he asked.

So he wanted to see her again? That was a good sign. At least, they seemed to be on the same page. "Not much. I got some shopping done yesterday. Did you need me to hostess another tasting?"

"Actually, I plan to scout around the downtown area and check out a few properties that are for sale. We plan to open a nightclub later this year, and there's a board meeting next week, so I'd like to have a few ideas to report, as well as some numbers. I realize you're not interested in real estate, but I thought I'd tap into your artistic and creative side."

It wasn't often that someone asked her opinion, especially when it came to business deals, especially real estate ventures. And the fact that Carlo had—and that he acknowledged her creativity—made her heart swell. "I'd love to go with you."

"Even to check out properties that are for lease or sale?"

"Believe it or not, that sounds like fun."

Carlo laughed. "Does anything not sound fun to you?"

"I'm not big on root canals—or dental visits in general."

"I'll make a mental note."

She turned to face him, still reluctant to get in her car and leave. As their gazes met, something passed between them. Something too big and powerful to ignore.

Carlo must have felt it, too, because he slipped his arms around her and drew her close. She suspected he intended to kiss her, which sounded a lot more fun than anything else he'd ever suggested.

When he lowered his mouth to hers, she closed her eyes and held on for what she suspected would be the ride of her life.

Chapter Six

Over the years, Carlo had experienced plenty of kisses, but he'd never had one quite like this. It began slowly and shyly, as he and Schuyler tested the sexual waters. But within a couple of heartbeats, it deepened and exploded with passion.

Schuyler leaned into him, and he pulled her close. Yet try as he might, he couldn't seem to get her close enough. While his hands caressed her back, exploring her curves and the slope of her hips, he relished her sweet taste, the floral scent of her shampoo and the feel of her in his arms.

He was never going to be content just spending the cocktail hour or a romantic dinner with her. Somehow, some way, he had to convince her that they had to take this newfound relationship to a deeper, more intimate level.

Of course, with the way she was kissing him back, convincing her wasn't going to take much effort on his part. Their mating tongues had kicked things up more than a notch already.

A car door opened and shut, bringing Carlo back to reality—if not his senses. He didn't especially care who'd caught them wrapped in a heated embrace, only that they'd been forced to stop.

With reluctance, he withdrew his lips from hers, glanced over his shoulder and spotted his father getting out of his car. Even in the waning light, he clearly saw the grin on his old man's face, one that shouted, *Attaboy, Carlo.*

"Good evening!" Esteban Mendoza's jovial tone damn near echoed through the vineyard. "I came to see how the tasting turned out, but by the look of things, I suspect it went especially well."

Carlo was never going to live this down. His father had been a ladies' man for years, maybe before his parents had actually divorced, although that was just his speculation. Either way, Esteban could appreciate the kind of kiss that was sure to spark a romantic liaison.

Schuyler, who seemed completely undaunted by the unexpected interruption, tossed his father a carefree grin. "I think it's fair to say everyone had a good time."

"Apparently." Esteban made his way closer, his smile deepening.

But then again, did Carlo even care what his old man thought, or what he might mention in front of his brothers? He was proud to have Schuyler in his arms. And if his luck held, in his bed.

"I certainly enjoyed the tasting this evening." Schuyler turned to Carlo, her eyes boasting an impish glimmer. "How about you?"

Whose side was she on? "I'd have to admit that it was probably the best I've had to date."

"That sounds promising." Esteban's smile widened. "I hope I didn't interrupt your…um…debriefing."

"Not at all," Schuyler said. "We're finished with that, and I was just leaving."

That's what she'd said, although Carlo wasn't ready to call it a day. Or rather, a night. And he'd hoped that the kiss they'd just shared might have changed her mind.

"Then I'll leave you to your goodbyes." Esteban pointed toward the new restaurant. "I'm going to see how things are going at La Viña."

As his father walked away, Carlo turned to Schuyler. "Should I apologize?"

"For what?"

Kissing her had been his first thought. Being caught had been his second. And his father's interruption of a heated moment came third. But she didn't seem to be the least bit concerned about any of it.

"I'm not going to dance around the issue," he said. "I like you, Schuyler. A lot. And there's definitely some mutual attraction at play."

"I won't argue that."

"Then why don't we let things play out between us and see what happens?"

She laughed. "I thought that's what this kiss was all about. And just for the record, I thought it played out nicely."

So it had.

"We clearly have chemistry," she admitted. "And I'm not at all opposed to seeing where a little romance might lead. But I'd hate to complicate things."

He supposed that she was talking about their working relationship. It was also possible that she was concerned about her upcoming introduction to some of the Fortunes who were in the inner circle. But he wasn't about to renege on the deal they'd made—even if a short-term affair didn't work out.

"We've both admitted that we're not interested in a serious relationship," he said. "So we can certainly keep things light and easy. And fun."

"Now, that's an interesting thought."

He figured she'd like that idea, since she'd made no secret of having a playful side.

"Why don't you sleep on the idea?" he suggested. "We can talk more about it tomorrow."

She blessed him with a bright-eyed smile that nearly lit the evening sky. "That works for me."

It definitely worked for him, too.

He kissed her one last time for the road. And to give her more romantic fodder to sleep on.

When Carlo drove into the porte cochere at the entrance of the Monarch Hotel, Schuyler was seated on a wrought iron bench near the valet desk, a disposable Starbucks coffee cup in her hand and that big black Chanel purse resting beside her.

That morning she'd pulled her hair up into a messy but stylish topknot and wore a red long-sleeve T-shirt, snug black jeans and running shoes. The moment she spotted his car, she flashed a happy grin and got to her feet.

Before either Carlo or the valet could get the door for her, she opened it herself and slid into the passenger seat, clearly eager to set out on their latest adventure.

But heck, so was Carlo.

As her breezy scent, something soft and floral, infiltrated his car and invaded his senses, he said, "I didn't expect you to be ready, but I'm glad you are."

"I'm always ready for an adventure."

Apparently so. For some reason, he'd assumed a pretty, stylish and wealthy woman like her would relish her beauty rest and take her time getting ready in the morning. But it hadn't taken Carlo long to realize Schuyler was unpredictable and not at all like other women.

He liked that about her.

In fact, when it came to Schuyler Fortunado, there was a lot to like. And he wasn't just counting those luscious blond locks, sparkling blue eyes and soft pink lips that could kiss a man senseless. She had an effervescent personality that kept him interested, intrigued. And completely engaged.

A man who had preconceived ideas about romance could find himself at a disadvantage with her. If he expected to tie her down in any way, he'd risk being disappointed or hurt. And if the poor guy thought he'd fallen in love with her, he might just convince himself that he actually liked having his life turned upside down.

Carlo would have to stay on his toes around her,

although he really wasn't worried. He always kept his romantic relationships lighthearted and simple.

As he pulled onto the city street, she asked, "Where are we going first?"

"I heard about an old bank building downtown that's vacant and for sale. It will need renovating, but it might have a lot of potential as a nightclub."

"Are you meeting the listing agent?" she asked.

"No, not this time. I'm just scouting the area before reporting back to the family."

"When you're done with the preliminary footwork, and if you decide to check out that property, you should consider calling my sister. Maddie works out of the Houston office, but she's really good at negotiating commercial deals. And while you could work directly with the seller's agent, the buyers should have someone who can watch out for their best interests."

Carlo had planned on getting an agent to represent the family. If he still lived in Florida, where he had a lot of contacts and connections, he'd know just who to call. But he hadn't researched any of the local agencies yet.

Still, Schuyler's suggestion was sound. Fortunado Real Estate had a solid, statewide reputation, with offices in Houston, San Antonio and Austin.

"I just might call your sister," he said. "But I have a question for you. Why didn't you suggest that I call your father?"

"No reason, really. My dad is the best commercial Realtor in the state, if not the entire country. But he's pretty busy."

"That's not surprising. He's built an impressive company."

"That's true, although my mom would like him to slow down, if not retire."

"For health reasons?"

"No, that's not it."

Schuyler had made no secret of the man's financial success, so Carlo assumed his wife would like him to enjoy the fruits of his labor.

"My dad worked very hard to build the company, so he's reluctant to pass the baton. But there's no reason he can't slow down some. My sister could run things blindfolded and with her hands tied behind her back."

"Do you think he'll eventually let her take over?"

Schuyler shrugged. "My mom would love that, but who knows?"

She grew silent as Carlo drove to the downtown area. He wasn't sure what Schuyler was thinking about. Her family and the successful empire her father had built, he supposed.

As his own thoughts drifted to finding the right property, making a good deal and jumping into the renovations, his enthusiasm soared.

Going to work with Alejandro and his brothers had been a smart move for him, a good one in which he'd found his true calling. He had a growing fervor to help build the winery and to expand the family's interests.

When he left Miami, he'd hoped that would happen, but he hadn't been sure it would. In the past, his initial passion for a project would peak then wane, and after a while, he'd become disenchanted and bored.

The same could be said for his love life, he supposed. After dating a woman for a couple of months, he'd lose interest in her, too.

He shot a glance across the seat at Schuyler, who was watching the city skyline, her eyes aglow. There was something special about her, something vital that sparked his excitement.

A smile tickled his lips. He had a feeling that he wasn't going to lose interest in this woman anytime soon.

As he pulled in front of the empty three-story brick building that had once housed a bank, he pointed it out to Schuyler.

"Wow," she said. "You were right. This place has a lot of potential."

That's what Carlo had thought when he'd first checked out the pictures on the internet and researched its history. "It was originally built in the mid-1880s and then renovated in the 1920s. But when the depression hit, it closed down."

"Has it been vacant all that time?"

"No, it's had several owners since then. It's also housed various offices and businesses. A couple years ago, a guy bought it with the intention of turning it into a trendy restaurant, but he died before finishing it. There were some legal issues when his heirs divided the estate, but from what I understand, the property is going on the market soon."

"I think you ought to snatch it up," Schuyler said. "What an awesome location for a nightclub. My mind is abuzz with ideas. I can't wait to see the interior."

Carlo felt the same way. His mind was spinning with the possibilities, too. And interestingly enough, he wanted Schuyler to be with him when he got his first look inside.

Maybe it was time to call Maddie Fortunado. But talk about complicating things. All he needed was to be knee-deep in a real estate negotiation with Schuyler's sister when—not *if*—their romantic relationship went south.

But he wouldn't let things become so involved that there'd be a blowup when they parted ways. Besides, they'd already decided to take things slow and easy.

Of course, if he kissed her again, things could escalate faster than either of them anticipated. But would that be bad?

Not unless he didn't handle their breakup well and things went up in smoke at the end.

"What other properties are you considering?" Schuyler asked.

With her sudden interest in the bank property, you'd never have known she'd been reluctant to work with her father's company. But then again, family dynamics could be difficult for outsiders to understand.

"There's an old warehouse about a mile from here," he said. "It has a lot of potential, too, but I'm not thrilled with the location. It's a little too far away from downtown."

"You might be surprised when you see it," she said.

"I agree."

Carlo took her to see that property, as well as another that was located a bit farther outside town. But they both came to the conclusion that the bank property would work best—if it went on the market. And if they could negotiate a good price.

As they left the last warehouse, Carlo was about to suggest they drive back to town and have lunch at a new café that had opened up across the street from her hotel, when Schuyler stiffened, pointed out the passenger window and yelled, "Stop."

"What's the matter?"

"I need to get out."

Stunned, he pulled to the side of the road. Had she gotten sick?

While the engine idled, Schuyler opened the door, jumped from the car and hurried across a vacant lot. He glanced in the rearview mirror, then turned in his seat and looked over his shoulder. He watched as she approached a big scraggly bush, its branches and leaves rustling.

She knelt down on the dried grass, as if paying homage to the wild shrub, and patted her hands on her thighs. Moments later, a scruffy little dog crept out from its hiding place, followed by another mutt that looked just like it.

Strays, he suspected. Was that why she'd wanted to stop?

She cooed to the small critters, then reached out to pick them up. Once they were both balanced in her arms, she carried them back to the car.

Seriously? What did she plan to do with them?

Now, there was a silly question. Obviously, she was

bringing them back to his car for a reason. And not one he was likely to appreciate.

Upon her approach, she called out, "Can you please get the door for me?"

He had half a notion to object, but instead, he leaned over, reached across the seat and opened it for her.

"Look what I found. Puppies. Two of them. And just look at the sweet little things. They're darling."

Actually, they were dirty and scrawny. And flea-bitten, no doubt.

"Can you believe someone would just drop them off on the side of the road like that?" she asked.

Actually, he could believe it. It wasn't right, but some people abandoned animals all too often. "What are you going to do with them?"

"If I can't find a home for them, I'm going to keep them."

His brow lifted. "You're staying in a hotel, remember? And I don't think a place as nice as the Monarch is going to let you keep them there."

"I know. But we can't leave them here."

Carlo had to agree, even though he wasn't what you'd call a dog lover. Sure, he and his brothers had pets as kids, but once they'd gotten into high school, their interests had turned to sports and girls.

He shot a glance across the seat, wondering what the dirty critters would look like once they had a bath. One pup, the smaller of the two, licked Schuyler's cheek. A love offering for being rescued, it seemed.

Apparently, she'd interpreted the doggie kiss the same way he had because she said, "Aw, sweetie, you're welcome. I wasn't going to leave you back there to starve to death or get hit by a car."

"What if the hotel won't let you keep them?" he asked.

"I'll think of something."

Hopefully, she didn't expect him to take them. His life wasn't conducive to caring for pets, for pooper-scoopers and walks in the park. Besides, he lived in a high-rise apartment that probably wasn't any more dog friendly than the Monarch.

"You'd better come up with a plan B," he said.

"I know." She grew somber for a moment, then said, "They've got to be hungry—and thirsty. I'm going to have to find a place that sells dog food."

"They're also in need of a good bath. And a flea dip. I suspect that a place that works with pets will have food and water for them, too."

"Then I'll have to find a groomer."

No wonder her family found her a bit on the impulsive side. But she clearly had a big heart, and he had a hard time finding fault in her for that.

As he headed back to the city, he picked up his iPhone, brought up Siri and said, "Directions to the nearest pet groomer."

When Siri responded with the name of The Pampered Fido, Schuyler got on her own smartphone and called to see if they had any openings today—and sooner, rather than later. As luck would have it, they could fit in both dogs if they came now.

"I hate to have you drive me all over town," Schuyler

said. "Do you have time to drop off the dogs and then take me back to the Monarch?"

"I'll make time." Otherwise, she and those dirty pups would be turned away before they could step foot onto the hotel premises. And where would that leave Carlo?

Besides, as much as he'd like to deny it, he had a heart, too. Not just for animals, but for pretty blondes who were more impetuous and loving than they ought to be.

Still, he had to admit this was a first. No other woman he'd ever dated, including Cecily, his ex-wife, would have been able to talk him into driving dirty, stinky dogs to the pet groomer. But hell, for some reason, he found himself on a constant adventure with Schuyler. One that, in her words, sounded like fun.

For the next ten minutes, Carlo followed the directions Siri gave him. At the same time, Schuyler juggled the pups in her arms while fiddling with her smartphone.

"What are you doing?" he asked.

"I think you were right about the Monarch Hotel, so I've been looking for a small studio apartment that's pet friendly and will allow me to sign a month-to-month lease."

So she planned to extend her stay in Austin, at least for the time being. He supposed that was good. He couldn't very well expect her to continue being a hostess for his special wine tastings while staying in a hotel. Besides, a month-to-month lease made good sense financially—no matter how healthy her trust fund might be.

And since she wasn't making a permanent move,

it suggested that she considered their relationship—either working or otherwise—to be temporary. And that meant she and Carlo were both on the same page.

"Are you having any luck?" he asked her a few minutes later.

"Actually, I am. There's an intern in my dad's Austin office who's been helping me, and he just found the perfect place." She slipped her phone into her bag, then glanced up at him and bit down on her bottom lip. "I'm sorry. I'm not trying to monopolize your day or take advantage of you. Once we drop off the dogs at The Pampered Fido, you can take me back to the hotel."

"What are you going to do there?"

"I'll check out and take my own car to pick up the dogs. Then I'll move into my new digs."

Carlo had plenty he could do this afternoon, but for some crazy reason, he didn't mind spending more time with her. "As long as I can get to the winery before La Viña opens for dinner, I don't mind helping you and the pups get settled."

She blessed him with a grateful smile. "I really appreciate this."

"No problem."

Her expression grew serious, and he watched her for a moment as her brow furrowed. When she looked up, she blew out a little sigh. "I'll also need to pick up some dog food, chew toys and maybe a couple of pet carriers."

Hopefully, they'd have enough hours in the day to accomplish everything she needed to do. But she couldn't very well adopt two puppies without getting the proper supplies.

Carlo had planned to take her to lunch, but since time was of the essence, their eatery options were limited.

"I've got an idea," he said. "Why don't we pick up sandwiches at a deli and find someplace outdoors where we can eat?"

"A picnic? That sounds fun."

Carlo chuckled and slowly shook his head. "I think *fun* is your middle name, Schuyler."

"It probably should be."

No doubt. Then he continued the drive, feeling as though he'd just agreed to be her partner in crime.

And hoping he didn't live to regret it.

Chapter Seven

While Carlo waited in the car, Schuyler dropped off the two pups at The Pampered Fido to be bathed, dipped and groomed.

"My goodness." Trudy, the shop owner, reached for one of the dirty dogs. "They're a mess."

"I found them in an abandoned lot," Schuyler said. "I couldn't just leave them there."

"I'm glad you brought them to me. And that I was able to fit them in. But I can't groom them unless they've had their first round of shots and been seen by a vet."

"I'd planned to have them examined, but I haven't gotten around to it yet."

"You know," Trudy said, "there's a new veterinary clinic across the street. Dr. Mayfield just opened his practice and isn't very busy yet. I'm sure he'll be able to check them out for you today."

"I wonder how long that'll take. My friend is in the car and doesn't have a lot of time." Schuyler bit down on her bottom lip, wondering if she'd have to take a rain check on that picnic after all.

"You're in luck," Trudy said. "The vet has a real heart for strays and people who rescue them. I'm sure I can get him to examine the dogs. He's probably on his lunch hour and might come right over."

"That would be awesome."

Trudy made a phone call, then gave Schuyler a thumbs-up. "Dr. Mayfield will be here in five minutes. He also said their first exam and shots are free."

Schuyler hadn't expected to get a deal, but the gesture was nice. And it was a good way for the vet to get new patients.

"You mentioned that your friend was on a time schedule," Trudy said, "so if you need to go, the vet can examine them here. I'll give you a call if he has any issues or concerns."

"That's really sweet of you. I need to shop for pet supplies, plus I'm moving into a new place this afternoon."

"I'll need two hours for their doggie makeovers," Trudy said. "You won't recognize these little guys when you come back."

"How much do I owe you?" Schuyler asked.

"Not a thing. Their first grooming is on me. I'll even feed them while you're gone."

The smallest pup whined as Schuyler walked out the

door, but she continued to Carlo's car, knowing they'd be in loving hands.

Once she climbed in, he started the engine and glanced across the seat. "Are you ready for lunch?"

"I'm hungry, but I think it would be best if we picked up the puppy supplies first."

"Sounds like a plan." Before backing out of the parking space, Carlo asked Siri for directions to the nearest pet supply store, which turned out to be a ten-minute drive from the groomer.

Once they arrived and began walking down the aisles, it took Schuyler another ten minutes to find everything on her mental shopping list. Only trouble was, one cart wasn't enough, and Carlo had to retrieve a second cart to fit everything she wanted to buy.

As they stood at the register, Schuyler turned to Carlo. "I can't believe you're being such a good sport about this. If the men in my family had to follow me around a store, especially one like this, they would have moaned and groaned about it."

"To be honest, I usually avoid going to malls or stores with women. In my experience, they tend to lollygag and ponder their purchases way longer than necessary, which only makes me grumpy. And then afterward, they can't seem to figure out why I'm in a bad mood."

"When I go to a store, I don't mess around. I make quick decisions." Too quick, if you asked her father.

Schuyler studied Carlo carefully, that dark hair a woman could run her hands through, those sparkling brown eyes, that dazzling smile. No sign of a bad mood there. And he hadn't uttered a single groan or moan.

She nudged him with her elbow and gave a little wink. "Apparently, going shopping with me doesn't make you the least bit grumpy."

"That's not surprising. I was more in awe than anything. You zoomed through this store like you were on a television game show, competing in a winner-take-all shopping spree."

She laughed. "See? Like I told you before, you've been dating the wrong women."

He winked back at her. "You might be right about that."

For a moment, she wondered if they'd stumbled onto a good thing, a special relationship that might last longer than a few weeks. Either way, they seemed to have become friends. Teammates, even. And that realization sent a little thrill right through her.

In the past, she would have been tempted to put on the brakes, but with Carlo… Well, the thought of nurturing whatever it was they'd found struck a chord. She felt almost hopeful.

But just in case her thoughts took a wrong turn, she reminded herself that Carlo had made it very clear that he wasn't into long-term relationships. And that he didn't make romantic commitments.

Schuyler didn't make them, either. Maybe that's why she felt good about this. About them.

Carlo would make the perfect fling. Yet something else niggled at her, causing her to question her long-held beliefs. He might also be the one man who could change her mind about what she wanted out of a romantic relationship, what she needed. And that might lead to disaster.

As the clerk bagged the last of her purchases—two doggie beds—Schuyler studied the carts loaded with the bagged items and scrunched her brow. "Uh-oh."

At that, Carlo laughed. "What's the matter? Now that you're calculating the cost, are you having a little buyer's remorse?"

"No, it's not that. I'm just worried that we can't fit all of this stuff in your car."

"I have a good-size trunk. And a backseat."

"Oh, good. That's a relief. I didn't want to have to put anything back."

He laughed. "Those two strays must think they died and went to doggie heaven. They've gone from rags to riches in one lucky day. Now they'll have everything a mutt could ever want."

Schuyler handed her credit card to the clerk, then turned to Carlo and slapped her hands on her hips. "Are you making fun of me and my new pets?"

"No, not at all. In fact, I'm enjoying this more than I'd expected. But for a while, I thought we'd need a third cart. And I wondered if we'd have to make two trips to lug all this loot back to the Monarch."

"Um… You know what?" She looked up at him and smiled. "We might have to make two trips to my new place, though. I've done some shopping, and my new suitcases alone are going to fill my trunk."

He glanced at his wristwatch. "Unless your studio apartment is clear across town, and you drag your feet until we have to deal with rush-hour traffic, I should be able to make it back to the winery before the dinner hour—and with time to spare."

If they'd been in Houston, Schuyler would have known the best route to take, but she wasn't the least bit familiar with Austin and could only relate what she'd been told. "According to my dad's intern, my new place is about ten minutes from the hotel."

"Then we should be fine."

That was good to know. She didn't want him to be late for work.

When the clerk returned her credit card, Schuyler pushed one cart out of the store, while Carlo pushed the other.

"If we run late," she said, "and it looks like you can't get back to the winery on time, I'll take a rain check on that picnic in the park."

"We'll see how things work out. But if we can't find time to eat, then maybe we can have that picnic at the winery tomorrow or the next day."

"That would be awesome. But can I bring the dogs?"

"Seriously?"

"Absolutely. I'm not going to be an irresponsible pet owner."

Carlo froze in his steps and studied her as if she'd placed a bird's nest on her head.

"Uh-oh," she said. "Don't look at me like that."

"Like what?"

"Like you've just lumped me in with all the women you date—the boring and predictable ones."

A slow smile slid across his face, and he reached out and cupped her jaw. "No way, Schuyler. You might

Dear Reader,

IT'S A FACT: if you answer 4 quick questions, we'll send you **4 FREE REWARDS!**

I'm not kidding you. As a leading publisher of women's fiction, we value your opinions… and your time. That's why we are prepared to **reward** you handsomely for completing our mini-survey. In fact, we have 4 Free Rewards for you, including 2 free books and 2 free gifts.

As you may have guessed, that's why our mini-survey is called **"4 for 4".** Answer 4 questions and get 4 Free Rewards. It's that simple!

Thank you for participating in our survey,

Pam Powers

To get your 4 FREE REWARDS:
Complete the survey below and return the insert today to receive 2 FREE BOOKS and 2 FREE GIFTS guaranteed!

◄ DETACH AND MAIL CARD TODAY! ▼

"4 for 4" MINI-SURVEY

1 Is reading one of your favorite hobbies?
☐ YES   ☐ NO

2 Do you prefer to read instead of watch TV?
☐ YES   ☐ NO

3 Do you read newspapers and magazines?
☐ YES   ☐ NO

4 Do you enjoy trying new book series with FREE BOOKS?
☐ YES   ☐ NO

YES! I have completed the above Mini-Survey. Please send me my 4 FREE REWARDS (worth over $20 retail). I understand that I am under no obligation to buy anything, as explained on the back of this card.

235/335 HDL GMYE

FIRST NAME	LAST NAME

ADDRESS

APT.#	CITY

STATE/PROV.	ZIP/POSTAL CODE

surprise me at times, and maybe even exasperate me, but I'd never lump you in with anyone. You're in a class all by yourself."

She'd never had a compliment like that, one that praised her uniqueness. A gush of warmth filled her chest.

"I'm touched," she said. More than he could possibly know. But the years she'd spent trying to explain and defend herself and her uniqueness brought out the skeptic in her. Rather than question him or herself, she nodded toward his car. "Let's get out of here. I'd like to squeeze in that picnic with you today. And as my hero, John Wayne, would say, 'We're burning daylight.'"

"So you're a John Wayne fan?" he asked, falling into step beside her.

"Glammy was. And since I used to watch a lot of Westerns with her, I liked him, too."

"The Duke was definitely a hero," he said.

That was true, but right now, Carlo seemed to be Schuyler's hero. And she wasn't sure if she should embrace that thought or run for the hills.

While Carlo waited for Schuyler to check out of the Monarch Hotel, he talked to the valet who'd brought up her Beamer from the garage and asked about their pet policy.

"Service dogs are okay," the young man said. "But the management really frowns on pets."

That's what Carlo had thought. But since Schuyler had already found another place to stay that would allow her to keep those puppies, she'd managed to circumvent the problem. And he found that to be interesting. She might be quirky, fun-loving and a bit impulsive at times, but she also seemed to think things through.

Just as the valet brought up her car, Schuyler exited the hotel, along with a bellman pushing a loaded luggage cart. While she tipped both men, Carlo helped them put everything in her trunk. Then he followed behind her car on the drive to her new, temporary residence, which was located on a tree-lined street in what appeared to be a quiet neighborhood.

He parked behind her along the curb in front of an older two-story brick home. They both got out of their cars, and he followed her to the front door.

"My place is in back," she said, as she rang the bell.

Moments later, a gray-haired woman wearing a blue-and-green muumuu and pink slippers answered the door. All the while, a big orange tabby cat threaded in and out of the woman's legs.

Schuyler introduced herself, and the woman reached out her hand in greeting. "I'm Dorothy Coggins, but you can call me Dottie."

"It's nice to meet you," Schuyler said. Then she turned and introduced Carlo as her friend. "He's helping me move in."

"Isn't that nice? And he's a good-lookin' fella to boot."

Schuyler glanced at Carlo and gave him a little wink. "That he is. Lucky me."

"That nice young man I talked to from the real estate office transferred the deposit and the first month's rent into my bank account. He looked over the lease I emailed him and said you'd sign it when you got here."

Once the paperwork was taken care of, Dottie lifted her arm, which sported a key connected to a red stretchy band around her wrist. She removed it and handed it to Schuyler. "Here you go." Then she stooped down and lifted the fat cat into her arms. "This is Rusty, our resi-dent mouser."

"Aren't you a sweetie," Schuyler said, as she stroked the feline's head.

Dottie smiled, clearly pleased by the affectionate gesture, then she scanned their parked cars, her brow furrowed. "Where are the puppies?"

"They're at the groomer," Schuyler said. "As soon as I bring them home, I'll ring your bell so you can meet them."

A smile tugged at one side of Carlo's lips, and he slowly shook his head. He liked animals, but he doubted he'd ever become so attached to one that he'd introduce it to the people he'd just met. But it was nice to think that Schuyler and her new landlady had something in common.

Dottie seemed to be a real character, a bit like he'd imagined Schuyler's grandmother had been. Maybe that was why they seemed to hit it off so well—and so quickly.

"I suggest you follow the graveled drive to the back," Dottie said. "That way, it'll be easier for you to unload your things. And just like I told that nice young man from the real estate office, that apartment isn't much. But it's clean and fully furnished."

"I saw the pictures he sent me, Dottie. I'm sure it'll work out just fine."

Ten minutes later, Carlo had helped Schuyler unload her purchases and her luggage into the small studio apartment. Dottie had been right, it wasn't much to shout about, but it had been scrubbed clean. He just hoped Schuyler's new pets didn't tear the place apart. If they did, that "nice young man" would have to forfeit whatever deposit Fortunado Real Estate had paid.

Finally, as the afternoon sun began a steady descent in the west, they returned to the groomer for the dogs. The happy pups didn't look anything like they had when they'd been dropped off. Their black-and-white fur was no longer dirty and matted down. Instead, it was glossy and puffy.

"Dr. Mayfield said they appear to be in good health," the groomer said. "He thinks they're about four to five months old. He also left you his card."

Schuyler pocketed the vet's contact information. "I'd certainly use him again."

"He also thought they had some cocker spaniel in their genes—and a little terrier. I think they might even have a little poodle in them, although it's hard to say."

Carlo hated to admit it, but the darn little mutts were actually cute. And those matching red collars fit perfectly.

"Look at them," Schuyler said. "Aren't they darling?"

"They do look a lot better now that they're clean," he admitted.

Schuyler turned to the groomer. "Thanks so much, Trudy. You did an awesome job."

"You're more than welcome. I hope you'll bring them back here for their next grooming."

"I'll definitely do that, although I'm not sure how long I'll be in town. I'm more or less a tourist. In fact, I have a couple of questions for you. Where's the nearest deli? And is there a park nearby where we can eat?"

"Well, there's a sandwich shop a few doors to the left. And there's a dog-friendly park about two blocks down from that and across the street."

"Great." Schuyler glanced at the clock hanging on the wall. "That'll work out perfectly. Thanks so much."

"Have you thought about what you're going to name the pups?" Trudy asked.

"I was going to call one of them Scruffy, but that was before their baths. I think Fluffy is more fitting now."

Trudy chuckled. "Since that little one really packed away his puppy food, you might want to call him Stuffy."

Schuyler laughed. "I like that. But maybe I'll shorten it to Fluff and Stuff."

After taking Trudy's business card, Schuyler placed both pooches on the sidewalk and let them try out their new leashes. But unfortunately, the neglected pups didn't like being under submission to humans. They each pulled this way and that, eager to go in different directions—and not to the left, where the sandwich shop was located.

"When it comes to training those dogs," Carlo said, "you're going to have your work cut out for you."

"Maybe so. But I think these little guys are going to turn out to be very bright. Besides, other than being a hostess at those special tastings you set up, I have plenty of time on my hands."

Actually, Carlo might just take up some of that free time himself.

"Why don't you let me carry Stuff." Carlo stooped and picked up the smallest pup. "Like you and the Duke said, 'We're burning daylight.' And I'd like to enjoy a little time in the park before I head to the winery."

"Good idea. I'm really hungry."

Fifteen minutes later, with their sandwiches, chips and sodas packed in two white sacks, they arrived at a small grassy area that wasn't quite what Carlo would call a park, although it had several picnic tables and a very small playground. It also had a green dispenser that provided plastic baggies. "So that's what Trudy meant by saying this park was dog friendly."

"I guess so. And it looks like we're the only ones here."

Carlo nodded to an empty table near a water fountain. "Should we sit there?"

"Yes, that's perfect." When she reached the spot, she placed Fluff down on the grass.

The critter didn't seem to mind its leash now, as it sniffed around, checking out its surroundings. Carlo set Stuff down next to Fluff.

While he removed the food from the sacks, Schuyler reached into her Chanel bag and pulled out several wipes. "Here. Now we can clean our hands."

"Thanks." He wondered what else she carried in that big bag. "Apparently you think of everything."

"I try."

He liked that about her. Hell, he liked too damn much about her. If pressed, he could probably create a list of things as long as the park bench on which they sat.

That ought to bother a man who'd made up his mind to keep his relationships simple and unencumbered, but that philosophy didn't seem quite as ingrained in him as it was before he'd met Schuyler.

He glanced at the tabletop, where someone had carved initials. He traced the letters with his finger. *B.K. Loves R.L.*

Who had defaced the public property in the attempt to proclaim his or her affection? A starry-eyed teenager? Or someone old enough to know better?

When it came to love, Carlo had been there, done that and bought the souvenir shot glass. So he was certainly old enough to know better.

Or was he? Each time Schuyler smiled at him, flashing those cute little dimples, or whenever he caught the soft lilt of her laugh, he found himself wondering if…

Now *that* was troubling. What in the hell was Schuyler doing to him? It was as if he'd morphed into a guy he no longer knew.

He scanned the small grassy area where they ate, then glanced at the table again, at the turkey sandwiches, half-eaten and resting on paper napkins, at the two cans of soda pop—root beer and black cherry.

Carlo enjoyed fine wines and classy restaurants. He didn't do parks or picnics. Yet here he was, listening to Schuyler tell a story about the time she and her beloved but eccentric grandmother made a trip to an animal shelter in Houston.

"Glammy told me she just wanted to look at the puppies and maybe play with the kitties in what she called the cat house. But when we entered the office and she spotted a three-legged cat and a one-eyed dog in the office, she was toast."

"What'd she do? Adopt them and take them home?"

Schuyler nodded. "That's exactly what she did. Their numbers were up, and they were going to be put to sleep at the end of the day. So Glammy adopted them herself. She called them Tripod and Pirate. I thought it was pretty cool, but my dad couldn't understand why she'd want to pour her love and attention on a couple of old, defective animals. But I don't think he ever really understood her need to make some kind of difference in the world. Instead, he only saw her as *being* different."

Schuyler's eyes glistened with unshed tears, and Carlo found himself sympathizing with the damaged pets, the quirky grandmother and the little girl who'd loved and admired her Glammy.

As a flood of compassion swept through his chest, he found himself smiling and admiring Glammy, too. "I wish I could have met her. It sounds like she had a lot of pluck, as well as a big heart."

Schuyler gave a little laugh, one that sounded bittersweet. "She did. I wish you could have met her, too."

"Whatever happened to Tripod and Pirate?"

Schuyler let out a sigh. "I wish I could tell you that there was a moral to the story."

"What do you mean?"

"You know, like on Facebook? When a family rescues a dog, then it eventually alerts them to a fire or a burglar or pulls their drowning toddler out of the pool?"

Carlo nodded, although he wasn't a big Facebook fan. And on those rare occasions when he did check out his home page, he usually passed right over those kinds of posts.

"It would have been pretty cool to tell my dad that one of those pets saved Glammy's life, but Tripod nearly broke her neck. One day she was bringing in her groceries from the car, and Tripod dashed out the door, tripping her and causing her to fall down. Before she could get up and chase after him, he was hit by a car."

"Dang, that's terrible."

"I know. It was very sad, but he died instantly. And the vet insisted that he didn't feel any pain."

"And what about Pirate?"

Schuyler's lips quirked into a crooked grin. "He spent a lot of time in the proverbial doghouse, but she finally found him a new home after he chewed up her vintage white go-go boots."

"She booted the dog out?" Carlo asked. "No pun intended."

"At first, she only scolded him and sent him out into the backyard to sleep. She had a soft heart and would have forgiven him by morning, but he howled like one of the hounds of hell, and she was afraid he'd wake the neighbors. So she brought him inside. The next day, she gave him to a friend who lived in the country and needed a watch dog." Schuyler tossed her hair over her shoulder. "Still, you have to give Glammy credit for at least trying to give Pirate and Tripod a loving home and new leases on life."

Carlo glanced at the frisky little puppies whose luck had changed the moment Schuyler spotted them.

Was Carlo's luck about to change, too? He'd never thought he'd needed it to. Not after his and Cecily's divorce was final and he'd picked himself up, dusted himself off and created a new philosophy on romance and dating, which meant that a helpmate was no longer in his future.

But something told him a change was in the wings. What kind of change, he really couldn't say. And that possibility left him more than a little unbalanced.

Over the next week, Schuyler represented the Mendoza brand at several of Carlo's special tastings and at an industry-wide event that was held last night in one of the downtown luxury hotels. She consistently brought in new orders that increased business, and the entire Mendoza clan not only thanked her, they raved about the amazing job she was doing for them.

Yet it was Carlo's praise that pleased her the most. He always made a point of complimenting her efforts at the wrap-up of each event, but he really didn't need to say a word. While he observed her from the sidelines, she could read his appreciation in his supportive stance, in the tilt of his smile and in the intensity of his gaze as it focused on her every move. And that pretty much said it all.

He'd watched her the same way today, during an

afternoon tasting at the winery. Then he'd slipped out of the room with the last of the guests, leaving her alone.

Outside, Fluff and Stuff frolicked on the grass. She could see them through the big bay window that looked out at the sculpture garden, where they rolled around, nipping at each other. It was a game they liked to play.

She supposed she should take them home now, but she decided to first wipe up a small spill that had splashed on the bar. So she bent to retrieve a dampened cloth she kept on one of the shelves underneath.

Before she could straighten, a familiar male voice called out, "Hey."

She glanced up to see Carlo entering the room wearing a sexy grin, and her heart rumbled in her chest. She tamped down the sudden thrill at his return, offered him a breezy smile and called out a "Hey" right back to him.

"Thanks for another successful day," he said. "That group just placed over two thousand dollars in orders. Good job."

"You're welcome." It wasn't often that people took Schuyler seriously, so she appreciated it when someone did. Especially this particular someone.

Silence filled the room. Sometimes, when they faced each other like this—neither of them saying a word, his praise stoking her pride—they seemed to be tiptoeing around... What exactly? She didn't know for sure, and it was probably best that she not put too much thought into it. So she broke eye contact and wiped down the marble-topped bar, even though it no longer needed it.

Still, she couldn't keep the thoughts from churning

in her mind. They'd talked about making love. At least, they'd done so indirectly. But so far they'd shared only a few heated kisses.

Sure, they flirted with each other when no one was around, but they'd yet to take that extra step. She was ready, though. She just hadn't done anything to instigate it.

And why was that? She'd never had trouble taking a bold step before. She'd never sat on the sidelines when something needed to be done. But she'd never actually made a brazen sexual move.

Schuyler might be quick to react at times, but for some reason, she was more cautious with Carlo. And there was good reason for it. He was a dyed-in-the-wool bachelor who only played at romance, and she knew better than to expect any more from him than fun and games.

Still, wasn't that what she'd wanted? A lighthearted fling while she was in Austin?

"You don't need to clean up," Carlo said, as he approached the bar where she worked. "The janitor will be here this evening."

"I know. I just want to wipe up a few splatters of spilled wine."

As he leaned against the bar, coming dangerously close as far as her hormones were concerned, she caught a whiff of his sea-breeze scent. Her heart rate, which was already escalated, slipped into overdrive. Dang, the guy did something to her. Something that made her hands tremble. But she'd be darned if she'd let the sexy Latino know that.

Attempting an unaffected pose, she reached under the bar, where she kept her purse, pulled out a pack of breath mints and held it out to him. "Would you like one?"

"No, thanks. I'm still enjoying the taste of the chocolate truffle I just stole from the kitchen."

"And you didn't think to bring one to me?"

"That was pretty thoughtless, huh?"

She chuckled. "Chef Bernardo ought to ban you from his territory for snatching so many snacks." She popped one peppermint mint into her mouth and replaced the rest in her bag.

Focus, she told herself. But that was hard to do when rebellious hormones were telling her brain to stand down.

As she retrieved the damp cloth she'd been using and swept it across the marble top one last time, her elbow brushed against a stack of paper cocktail napkins, causing them to flutter to the floor. "Oops."

She and Carlo bent at the same time to pick them up, and their hands met. Their fingers touched. Their gazes met and locked, setting off a flurry of pheromones that darn near knocked her for a loop.

Was she ready for this?

Yes, but what if things turned serious for her? It certainly wouldn't for him.

She really ought to laugh off their obvious attraction— or at least ignore it, like she'd been doing this past week.

Instead, she placed her hand on his jaw, felt the light

bristle on his cheek, and common sense turned to mush. Without any thought to the consequences, she drew his mouth to hers.

Chapter Eight

Carlo didn't know how many more heated kisses he could share with Schuyler before he completely lost his head and said something stupid, promised something he couldn't give her. But right now, all he could think to do was to wrap her in his arms and take each moment as it came.

So they knelt on the tasting room floor, hands caressing, tongues mating, breaths mingling. Yet the only tasting going on right now had uncovered a tantalizing blend of peppermint and chocolate. It was enough to make him want to eat her up, if not feel her up. And try as he might, he couldn't seem to get enough of this amazing woman.

As the kiss intensified, he wondered where they could steal away for a more private sexual exploration.

Before he could rack his brain for options, the door creaked open.

Dammit. Who'd caught them this time?

He slowly pulled his mouth away and turned to the doorway, where his father stood, that atta-boy grin lighting his eyes once again and shaving twenty years off his face.

"Apparently," Esteban said, "I've done it again. You must think I have lousy timing."

He had that right. Carlo might be frustrated by the interruption, but he certainly wasn't embarrassed by it. His old man wasn't, either. And judging by that twinkle in his eyes, he was getting a big kick out of it.

Too big, it seemed. Word of this was soon to hit the Mendoza rumor mill.

Schuyler, who seemed a wee bit more bothered by Esteban's arrival this time than last, leaned back and combed her fingers through her hair. Then she reached for a handful of napkins on the floor. "Carlo was helping me pick up the mess I made."

"I can see that." Esteban winked at Carlo. "I've taught my sons to always offer their assistance to a young lady in need."

The innuendo didn't go unnoticed, but there wasn't much Carlo could say at this point. Besides, he was too stunned by his growing attraction to Schuyler—and his growing desire to take her to bed.

Now, there was an idea. Once a relationship turned sexual, his interest in the woman began to dissipate, and he'd pull back. So if he and Schuyler actually made love, they just might be able to put this blasted attraction behind them and move on.

Not that he was the least bit tired of her yet. Nor was he ready to put any distance between them. But he wasn't at all comfortable with the skewed idea that kept cropping up. One that suggested he might actually be falling for her.

Schuyler hadn't made any secret of the fact that she liked to have fun. And she was just the kind of woman he'd like to play around with.

But it wasn't going to be the least bit fun if he let his feelings get in the way.

Esteban Mendoza couldn't keep his mouth shut if it was covered in duct tape, especially when he had four sons and a nephew to entertain.

Carlo had no more than entered the winery yard after Schuyler drove off with the puppies in her Beamer, when all the good-hearted but unwelcome teasing began.

"Hey, bro," Mark called out, a smirk plastered across his face. "Do I hear the sound of wedding bells in the distance?"

"Very funny," Carlo said.

Rodrigo laughed. "That's not the story we heard."

That wasn't surprising. His father had been connecting a lot of romantic dots that weren't there. At least, there wasn't anything going on until he and Schuyler actually addressed the issue—and pursued it.

"What pumped-up story did you hear?" Carlo asked his brother, although he had a darn good idea.

Rodrigo folded his arms across his chest, his grin rivaling that of the Cheshire cat. "Just that you and Schuyler were steaming up the windows in the tasting room."

It was hard to argue that. Still, Carlo shot a thanks-for-nothing glance at his father, who was an irrepressible flirt and a natural-born ladies' man.

"Better watch out," Chaz said.

Carlo shook his head. "You guys are making something out of nothing."

"That kiss on the tasting room floor wasn't the first one I saw," his father said. "And I damn sure wouldn't call either of them 'nothing.'"

"It's not what you think." At least, Carlo didn't want them to make that assumption. He glanced toward the restaurant, where Chef Bernardo was prepping the waitstaff before the dining room opened for dinner. He ought to attend that meeting, which gave him the perfect excuse for a quick escape.

"I'm glad to hear that kiss didn't mean a thing," Stefan said. "I assume that means I'm free to hit on Schuyler. I've always been attracted to petite blondes, especially one with a great personality, big blue eyes and sexy curves. And if she's free for the taking, I wouldn't mind making a move."

Carlo stiffened. He loved his brothers. He really did. But he didn't want any of them staking a claim on Schuyler. Not yet, anyway. And maybe not ever.

"Okay," he admitted. "There's a little something brewing between us. But I'm not sure what it is. And just so you know, Schuyler feels the same way I do about marriage and commitment."

"So it's just a drive-by romance?" Chaz asked.

It certainly should be. That was the plan.

"Hey," Carlo said, "even if there might be a little more than that going on, Schuyler lives in Houston. So it couldn't be more than a temporary thing."

Chaz placed his hand on Carlo's shoulder and gave it a brotherly squeeze. "For a divorced guy who swore off making any more romantic commitments, I'd say you're playing with fire."

There might be some truth to that statement. A part of him recognized that he could develop deep feelings for Schuyler, but he didn't like the thought of becoming vulnerable. So he shrugged it off and addressed the elephant in the winery. "You can't blame me for being gun-shy when it comes to long-term commitments."

He knew they'd all assume he was talking about his failed marriage, which was a good reason in itself. But on top of that, Carlo and his four brothers had grown up in an unhappy household.

Their father had traveled for business, but even when he was home he spent a lot of evenings with his friends. He might be stone sober now, but he'd had a drinking problem back then. Still, that was no excuse for prac-tically abandoning their mom and forcing her to raise the boys mainly on her own.

Needless to say, they'd fought a lot—over his ab-sence, his drinking and, while it was just speculation on Carlo's part, a little lipstick on Esteban's collar had probably been an issue, too. After each blowup, they'd make up, only to start the cycle all over again.

Carlo, who'd been the oldest, had a front-row seat

to the family drama. Sure, he'd known his parents had loved each other. They'd had moments of passion and affection interspersed with the arguing, but eventually his mom got tired of it and left his dad. Their divorce had taught Carlo a lesson about love.

"Just to keep the record straight," Carlo said. "There won't be any wedding bells for me."

At that, his cousin Alejandro, who'd just returned from a weeklong seminar in California, stepped forward. "I know how you feel."

Did he? Alejandro had recently married Olivia Fortune Robinson and was happier than he'd ever been.

"But you should give love a chance," Alejandro said.

Carlo had done that once. And it had blown up in his face. "Some people might be able to have a committed relationship, Alejandro. And you're one of them. But I'm not."

After his divorce, Carlo had poured himself into his work, managing restaurants and a nightclub in Miami. And his move to Texas hadn't changed that.

"Listen," he said, nodding toward La Viña, "I'd love to stay here and chew the fat with you guys, but I've got work to do."

Yet as he walked away, a beautiful blonde had him thinking about sexual fun and games. And he'd be damned if he'd let it become any more than that.

Formal invitations had gone out more than two weeks ago for the Valentine's party that would take place in just three short days, and the entire Mendoza family—at least those living in Austin and involved with the winery—had been busy, pulling out all the stops for what was sure to be an impressive event.

Carlo and Bernardo had put together a tantalizing menu. Esteban had negotiated a special deal with a talented string quartet to provide the music during dinner, as well as a popular local DJ for the dance to follow. And Alejandro, with the help of Carlo's brothers, was planning to go all out decorating the grounds and the restaurant.

True to his word, Carlo had announced that they would have a special wine tasting during the cocktail hour, and Schuyler would be the hostess. That would allow her to meet the many Fortunes who would be in attendance. Needless to say, she was delighted to have the opportunity to see up close and observe them in a social setting. So she'd offered to help with the party preparations.

The evening weather had been unseasonably temperate for February, and if it continued, they planned to hold the tasting in the sculpture garden.

Schuyler intended to bring the puppies with her to the winery today, which she often did. She liked giving them a chance to play outdoors. But Dottie, her landlord, had taken a real liking to Fluff and Stuff. She'd also been helpful in housebreaking them and teaching them to walk on a leash.

"When my Punky crossed the rainbow bridge," Dottie had said, "I swore I'd never get another dog. It's too painful to lose them. But these little rascals have made me reconsider that decision."

So it was no surprise when Schuyler was heading for her car, Dottie caught her in the yard.

"Oh." The older woman's smile faded. "You're leaving. I was going to invite you and the puppies to the dog park today. It's Bailey's birthday."

"Bailey?" Schuyler asked.

"You know, Donna Mae's Pomeranian mix? I introduced you to her last week, when we took Fluff and Stuff on a walk."

"Oh, yes." In Schuyler's defense, they'd met several dogs and owners along the way. "If you want to take them to the park, it's fine with me. But I could be gone until later this evening. Do you mind keeping an eye on them that long?"

"Not at all," Dottie said. "I used to take Punky to the park all the time. And I met a lot of really sweet people there. I miss not chatting with them, but after Punky died… Well, it was a little…tough."

"I understand." Schuyler handed her landlord the leashes. "Go ahead and take them. I'm sure you'll all have a great afternoon." Then she climbed into her car, knowing the pups were in good hands.

If she wasn't so determined to check things out for that Valentine's Day tasting, she might have gone with Dottie. She'd never attended a dog's birthday party, and it sounded like it'd be a hoot.

Twenty minutes later, as Schuyler arrived at the winery, she spotted several of the Mendozas' cars in the parking lot, including Carlo's. But she didn't see anyone milling about. She supposed she'd run into them soon enough. So she headed for the sculpture garden to determine the best place to set up the portable wine bar.

She'd no more than decided on a spot near the new fountain, when a car engine sounded out front. Curiosity got the best of her, and she went to see who'd arrived. She circled the perimeter of the tasting room, entered the yard and spotted three women getting out of a white late model Cadillac.

Schuyler didn't recognize the driver or the two others with her—a redhead in her twenties and a middle-aged brunette. Since no one else seemed to be around, she embraced her inner hostess and greeted them with a friendly smile.

"Hi there," she said. "Can I help you?"

The woman who'd been driving, a forty-something blonde who was professionally dressed in black slacks and a tailored white blouse, reached out her hand in greeting. "I'm Betsy Wilkins, a wedding planner with White Lace and Promises, and these are my clients, Joelle Pearson and her mother, Mavis."

Schuyler introduced herself, saying she worked for the winery, which was true, albeit temporarily.

"We've been checking out several possible venues," Betsy said. "But we haven't yet found a place that hits the mark. One of my colleagues mentioned that the Mendoza Winery might be scheduling special events in the near future, so I thought we'd drop by and see if we could get a tour of your property."

Schuyler would love to show them around and schedule the very first Mendoza Winery wedding, which would be a real feather in her cap. But she didn't want to step on anyone's toes.

Wow, now that was a first. She didn't often tamp down her enthusiasm—or the compulsion to act quickly. But she'd come to respect Carlo and his family. All of them—even Esteban, who'd assumed that she and Carlo were romantically involved and liked to tease them about it every chance he got.

"I'm a hostess for special...events," Schuyler said, pumping up her actual title. "I'd be happy to show you the property. And if we're lucky, we'll run into Alejandro or Carlo, who can provide even more details about the winery's calendar. When is the wedding?"

"Saturday, July eighteenth," the bride said. "I know we're getting a late start, but my fiancé and I are going to attend graduate school in August, and we want to get married here before we have to move."

"Congratulations on all counts," Schuyler said. "I'm not sure what you're looking for, but I have to tell you, if I were getting married, I'd love to have an outdoor ceremony here, followed by a dinner reception. Follow me, and I'll show you what I mean."

When she led them to the sculpture garden, the mother let out a little gasp of surprise. "This is lovely!" Then she turned to her daughter. "What do you think, honey?"

"I like it. And I love that fountain. The blue Spanish tile matches the color of the bridesmaids' dresses."

"There are a lot of possibilities," Schuyler said. "If you should decide on an evening ceremony, we can put up twinkly white lights on the trees."

"Oh," the bride said. "That's a great idea."

"We also plan to add a permanent gazebo in the very near future," Schuyler added.

Okay, so that wasn't entirely true. No one had mentioned anything to her about that, but she'd certainly push for one if the Pearsons decided to hold the wedding here.

"Why don't you come with me," Schuyler said. "I'll take you to see La Viña, our restaurant. And if we're lucky, I might be able to introduce you to Bernardo, our chef."

"That would be awesome," the bride said.

The women followed Schuyler. All the while, they chattered to themselves about guest lists, dinner menus and cake flavors.

When they entered La Viña, which had already been set up for the dinner hour, Mavis, the mother of the bride, made her way to the nearest window, which reached from the hardwood floor to the arched oak-paneled ceiling. "Oh my gosh. Would you look at that view of the vineyard?"

"It's absolutely gorgeous." Betsy reached into her purse, pulled out a business card and handed it to Schuyler. "I have several other clients who are also looking for a wedding venue. So I'll be calling you to set up a couple of tours in the next couple of weeks."

Schuyler hoped she wasn't overstepping her bounds, but Carlo had told her that he wanted her to be the winery hostess for special tastings. Maybe he'd also meant special events. At any rate, that would be her response when they broached the subject.

"If you'll give me a minute," Schuyler said, "I'll check and see if the chef is available to meet you."

Sure enough, when she entered the kitchen, Chef Bernardo was hard at work, seated at his desk and sketching out a list of some kind. But it was Carlo who caught Schuyler's eye.

He was dressed casually today in khaki slacks and a white button-down shirt, the sleeves rolled up his muscular forearms. When she approached, he turned away from Bernardo and flashed a dazzling smile her way. "Hey, I'm glad you're here. I wanted to go over a few things with you."

She was delighted to know he was as happy to see her as she was to see him. "Me, too. I was checking out the sculpture garden a few minutes ago and I had an idea to add twinkly white lights on the trees for the party. But before we get into that, I ran into some people you need to meet. They're in the dining room."

He scrunched his brow. "Who is it?"

"A bridal consultant and her clients. They're interested in having a wedding here in July."

"That's great. And the timing should work out perfectly—if they're interested in having it here." Carlo followed Schuyler through the swinging doors and back to the restaurant.

The women, who were still standing at the window gazing at the lush vineyard that grew on the hillside, turned around at their approach.

"Betsy," Schuyler said, "this is Carlo Mendoza, the vice president of the winery."

"It's nice to meet you." Betsy shook his hand. "We

were just marveling at the view. This would make a lovely backdrop for a wedding."

"Thank you," Carlo said. "You should check out the sculpture garden while you're here."

"We've already seen it. Your special event co-ordinator was very helpful. She also gave us some ideas to consider."

Schuyler stole a glance at Carlo, wondering how he would accept the title Betsy had given her. But he didn't even blink.

"Betsy is a wedding planner with White Lace and Promises," Schuyler added. "And these are her clients, Mavis and Joelle Pearson. Joelle is getting married in July."

Carlo moved toward the women, reached out and shook their hands. "It's nice to meet you. I'm glad you stopped by. And yes, we're scheduling special parties and events beginning in June."

"Do you have a brochure we can take with us?" Betsy asked.

"I'm afraid it's still at the printer," Carlo said. "We've just begun to take reservations."

Schuyler hadn't realized that they'd started booking events. But then again, she really wasn't privy to those kinds of things.

"Would your chef be willing to talk to us about pos-sible menus? We'd also like to set up a tasting for the bridal party."

"Absolutely."

"Great. We'll need to talk things over when we get

back to my office," Betsy said. "I'll let you know once we've made a decision."

"I've already made my decision," Joelle said. "I want to get married here. I want an evening wedding in the garden, with white lights adorning the trees, followed by a dinner reception."

"That can be arranged." Carlo reached into his pocket, pulled out a business card and gave it to Betsy. Then he and Schuyler followed them back to their car.

"We'll need a deposit to hold the date," Carlo told them. "Give me a call and I'll get you a contract with all the details."

"I assume that means we'll be working with Schuyler as your on-site coordinator." Betsy turned to Schuyler. "Can I have your card, too?"

Schuyler wasn't sure what to tell her. *I don't have any business cards because I was just blowing smoke when I told you my position with the Mendoza Winery.* Before she could come up with a response, Carlo spoke for her.

"Schuyler is a new hire," he said, "so her cards are still at the printer, along with the brochure."

Bless his heart. He'd played along with her white lie. She was so grateful, she could kiss him.

Of course, kissing him would only make things more complicated, since she had every intention of returning to Houston.

Or had her plans begun to shift?

She'd told him that she'd give lovemaking some thought. And she'd done just that. Day after day, she'd relived their heated kisses. And night after night, she'd slept on his suggestion to let passion run its course.

And each morning, she'd awakened to the same conclusion. They really should see how a short-term affair would pan out. Like it or not, she wanted to make love with Carlo.

Of course, becoming intimate could complicate their working relationship. Then again, her position at the winery was only temporary. So scratch that complication.

But there was also another consideration. She'd begun to feel more for Carlo than she'd felt for any other man. And while she'd never thought of herself as marriage material, she might reconsider a more serious relationship with a guy like him.

Carlo continued to charm the women as they discussed further details. Then, as they watched Betsy drive away with the Pearsons, he turned to Schuyler. Truthfully she was a bit nervous to hear what he had to say now that they were alone. Would he be angry at the way she'd inserted herself in winery business? She braced herself for a dressing-down. Instead, his face lit up with a smile.

"You're amazing."

Her heart soared at the compliment. "I am?"

"You're the perfect hostess for our tastings. And now you've pretty much locked in our first wedding. Betsy was obviously impressed." He slowly shook his head, that dazzling smile still stretched across his lips. "For a woman who's sworn off romance and marriage, you have a real knack for this sort of thing."

"Yeah. Well, a wedding celebration and a reception is just another kind of party, right?"

"Good point. Either way, I'm going to talk this over with Alejandro, but I think he'll agree to offer you a permanent position at the winery."

"Seriously?"

"Absolutely."

Wow. She hadn't seen that coming. Usually words like *permanent* made her want to cut bait and run. But she didn't feel that way now.

"Thank you," she said. "I'd have to think about that, but I don't mind you two talking it over."

"Good. I'm glad to hear that."

Was he? She hoped there was more to the offer than the service that Schuyler could provide the family business. Was he hoping to keep her around so they could strike up a romance?

"Have you seen *Jersey Boys*?" he asked, throwing her for yet another loop.

"No, but I love Frankie Valli and the Four Seasons."

"Good. It's playing at the Paramount Theater, and I have two tickets for the show next Saturday. Would you like to go with me?"

She'd have to ask Dottie to dog sit for her, but there wasn't anything she'd rather do than go out on a real date with Carlo. "That sounds like fun."

"Good. I'll pick you up around five o'clock so we can have dinner first."

"I'll be ready." That date was sounding better and better. Dinner and a show and…

She wondered if he'd be ready for a romantic wrap-up to their date. She certainly was.

Chapter Nine

The Valentine's Day party at the Mendoza Winery was sure to be everything Schuyler hoped it would be and more. It was also the kind of elegant event she would have loved to attend as an invited guest. But she was content to serve the Mendoza wines and discreetly observe the Fortunes.

As Carlo planned, the evening would kick off with a wine tasting in the sculpture garden so the guests could see the impressive improvements he and Alejandro had made to the property. Soon the winery would be bursting with happy chatter, but the only sounds now came from the water gurgling in the new fountain.

The sun had just set, and the white twinkling lights gave the grounds a festive and romantic ambience. There seemed to be a magical aura, too. As if something special was about to happen.

And wasn't it? Schuyler had dreamed about meeting some of her Fortune relatives, and she was about to do that tonight.

Alejandro had invited Mendozas galore to celebrate, and from the many RSVPs that had rolled in, it seemed that quite a few had jumped at the chance to attend. Several would be coming from Horseback Hollow, including Alejandro's brother, Cisco, and his wife, Delaney nee Fortune. Their sister Gabriella and her husband, Delaney's brother Jude Fortune Jones, would be traveling with them. Counting those from Red Rock—and the ones living in Austin—it would make a full house.

Schuyler might have read Ariana Lamonte Fortune's articles in *Weird Life* magazine, but she was afraid she wouldn't be able to keep everyone straight. Still, she'd do her absolute best to match every face to a name and remember every family connection.

Carlo had done his part to help her with that by giving her a primer on which Fortunes would be in attendance, although Schuyler wasn't sure she'd be able to pick them out of the crowd without his assistance.

Eager to see the Fortunes, she'd spent way more time getting ready than she usually did.

She'd worn her red dress tonight, which had both a scooped neckline and a low-slung back. It was stylish and flattering, and while she'd worn it before at other tastings, she thought it would be especially appropriate for Valentine's Day. Her hair was swept up into a stylish twist that revealed her diamond stud earrings, a birthday gift from her parents. And as a final touch, she'd used a bit more makeup than was her usual habit.

When she'd taken one last look in the mirror at home—or rather her temporary Austin residence, she'd been pleased with her appearance.

Taking a deep breath, she walked into the winery garden. She wanted to make a good impression tonight, even though she wouldn't introduce herself as Julius Fortune's granddaughter. Still, she was finally here—ready and eager for the night to unfold.

She was glad someone had already set up the portable bar, but the wines she'd be serving hadn't been brought out yet. She was just about to go inside the tasting room to get them when Ricardo, the man who hosted the daily tastings at the winery, came outside pushing a cart loaded down with wineglasses. He also brought out bottles of Sunny Days, a chenin blanc, and Desert Sunset, a Syrah.

She wasn't sure why he was here. Perhaps to pass out appetizers or serve dinner in the restaurant. Either way, she thanked him for setting things up.

"No problem," he said, as he uncorked the bottles.

"Are we serving any other wines tonight?" she asked.

"I'm not sure. Carlo specifically asked me to bring out this cart. But there's another one still in the tasting room. I'm going back for it. It's possible that he has a few others in mind."

Schuyler had yet to spot Carlo or any of his brothers. She assumed they were making last-minute preparations in La Viña. She was about to go in search of him, but when a car engine sounded out front, signaling that the guests had begun to arrive, her steps stalled.

She whipped out her cell phone, which held her Fortune family cheat sheet, and gave it one last read. It was impossible to ignore the Mendoza connections to them, which convinced her that she'd made the right decision by starting her quest at the winery distribution center in Austin Commons.

Okay, she told herself. *You've got this.*

Alejandro Mendoza, Carlo's cousin, was at the top of the list. He owned the winery and was married to Olivia Fortune Robinson. Interestingly enough, four of Alejandro's siblings were also married to one of the Fortune Robinson clan. Joaquin was married to Zoe, and Matteo was married to Rachel.

Several others of the Robinson Fortune clan would be here as well, including Ben and his wife, Ella, Wes and Vivian, Kieran and Dana, Graham and Sasha, Sophie and Mason... Wow. Would Schuyler be able to remember who belonged to whom?

It wasn't likely. Still, she was glad to have the chance to meet them all.

As the guests began to enter the garden, dressed to the hilt and ready to party, she couldn't help noting that all of the Fortunes and Mendozas were dazzling, good-looking and well dressed. It was an embarrassment of riches, both literally and figuratively.

She wasn't sure whom she should approach first. Not that she'd forget to be a hostess. In fact, she'd walk up to them and invite them over to the wine bar for a tasting. She peeked at her phone once more. She'd scanned only the first few names on her list when Carlo came over and placed an arm around her shoulders.

"Don't be so obvious," he said. "If you're not careful, people will become suspicious."

"I'll try, but this is a big night for me. And I'm a little nervous."

He stroked her back, his fingers resting on her bare skin, sizzling her with his touch. "I know you came to work this evening, but I'd rather you were a guest instead of an employee. So I asked Ricardo to cover for you."

Seriously? That was a sweet thought.

"How are you going to introduce me?" she asked.

He blessed her with a smile. "You're my date tonight."

Her heart spun like an ice skater about to score an Olympic gold medal, and she returned his smile with a confident grin. "I shouldn't have any problem pulling that off."

He drew her a little closer, and as she caught a tantalizing whiff of his sea-breezy cologne, she leaned into him. Pretending to be Carlo's date was going to be an easy role to play.

Ricardo, who'd just returned from the tasting room with the other cart, gave her a thumbs-up. "I'm back, Schuyler. I'll take it from here."

"Thanks." She turned to her handsome escort. It was nearly intoxicating to think of herself as his special lady. Would people think they were lovers? She wouldn't mind if they did.

Carlo looked great tonight in that stylish black suit, crisp white shirt and red tie. In fact, they matched so well, one might think they'd gotten dressed together.

"Come on," Carlo said, taking her by the hand. "I'll introduce you to some of our guests."

This was what she'd been waiting for, the chance to meet some of her cousins, and she had Carlo to thank for it. Yet her enthusiasm paled ever so slightly, making room for the swell of pride she felt at being with him all evening. His date. And, hopefully soon, his lover.

As they crossed the grass, Carlo squeezed her hand and whispered a soul-stirring compliment that bolstered any lack of confidence she might have had. "You look gorgeous tonight. I love that dress."

She brightened, and her heart took flight once more. The only thing he could have said that would have made her happier was that he loved *her*, but that didn't make sense. Why would something like that pop into her head? She shook off the silly thought as quickly as it crossed her mind.

They made their way over to Alejandro, who stood next to a pretty brunette. That had to be his wife. Schuyler had had the pleasure of meeting him only twice, since he'd been out of town all last week. But she'd been especially eager to meet Olivia, a bright young professional at her father's company, Robinson Tech. A woman who had no idea that she and Schuyler shared the same grandfather— good ol' Julius Fortune, who'd left a trail of illegitimate children in his wake.

Olivia had married Alejandro last year, and while her last name was now Mendoza, she was every bit a Fortune by birth. Just as Schuyler was.

Before Carlo could make any introductions, Alejandro reached out and shook Schuyler's hand. "I'm glad you're here. I want to thank you again for all you've done for us in a very short period of time."

"It was my pleasure," Schuyler said, reveling in the praise that made her sound like the Mendoza Winery employee of the week. "But to be completely honest, your wines practically sell themselves."

"I'm glad you like them." Alejandro turned to the brunette standing beside him. "Olivia, this is Schuyler Fortunado. For the past two weeks she's worked for us as a brand rep at Carlo's special tastings. And just a couple days ago, she scheduled our first wedding and reception."

"It's nice to meet you, Schuyler." Olivia extended her hand in greeting.

Schuyler took it, but a customary response balled up in her throat. And she'd be darned if she knew why. She never found herself at a loss for words and rarely suffered any insecurity. But dang. Olivia was one smart cookie. What if she saw through the fake-date thing? What if Olivia figured out who Schuyler was and why she was here?

Finally, in what seemed like forever but had been only a couple of beats, Schuyler rallied her senses, tamped down her worries and blurted out, "You have no idea how glad I am to meet you."

Okay, so that was way more truthful and sincere than she'd planned to be. She hadn't meant to sound like she was having a fangirl moment, but the thrill of meeting her Fortune cousin had just tumbled off her tongue.

Luckily, Olivia didn't seem to notice. Nor did she look the least bit suspicious about Schuyler having any ulterior motives. And even though Schuyler did, she didn't mean anyone any harm.

Moments later, two other brunettes bearing a striking family resemblance approached them, and Olivia introduced her sisters, Zoe and Rachel, to Schuyler.

This was so cool. In one fell swoop, Schuyler had met three of her cousins. Counting Nathan, the reluctant Fortune who lived in Paseo, that made four. But she didn't expect to see him tonight. He seemed to prefer living out in the boonies, which suggested that he wasn't very social. On top of that, she doubted that he and Bianca would want to make that long drive.

"If you ladies will excuse me," Carlo said, "Alejandro and I have a little business to discuss." He gave Schuyler's hand a gentle, reassuring squeeze before releasing his hold. Then the two men left her and her cousins to get better acquainted.

The three Fortune Robinson sisters, all of whom were stylish, beautiful and smart, chatted about normal things. Family things. And Schuyler hung on every word. She wasn't sure what she'd been expecting to learn when meeting them, but clearly some of the media accounts had been exaggerated—as they often were.

Maybe, if she played her cards right, they'd provide her with more information about the others who would be arriving soon.

Schuyler glanced across the garden, where Carlo and Alejandro stood. Did they really have something to talk about? Or had Carlo just given her another unexpected and thoughtful gift?

Girl talk with Olivia, Zoe and Rachel might prove to be sweeter and better than a pair of bunny slippers.

"What did you want to talk to me about?" Alejandro asked Carlo, as they crossed the lawn to a more private spot.

In truth, Carlo didn't have much to say that couldn't wait. He'd just wanted to give Schuyler some time to get to know her cousins. But that wasn't something he would admit.

"There were a couple of things I wanted to mention," Carlo said. "I didn't get a chance to tell you that, while you were at that seminar, I drove by a few properties that might work out for us if we go forward with that nightclub project."

"What'd you think of them? Did any of them have potential?"

Carlo related his thoughts and his opinions of all three. "I'm really interested in that bank building. It might be a little small, but we could expand it during a remodel."

"What's the asking price?"

"I have no idea. It hasn't been listed yet, and I haven't approached a real estate agent who can provide any comps. Schuyler suggested that we talk to her sister Maddie. If we want to go forward with this, I think that's probably a good idea."

Alejandro nodded his approval, then glanced over to where his wife, her sisters and Schuyler stood. Each smiling lady held a glass of wine and seemed to have found plenty to chat about.

"We lucked out when you stumbled upon Schuyler," Alejandro said.

"Yes, I know." But it wasn't just the Mendoza family business that had scored with her arrival. Carlo felt as if he'd lucked out, too. Of course, the jury was still out on that.

"Your father seems to think that you're serious about her," Alejandro said.

Was he? He hadn't planned things to get that deep, although he felt a lot more for her than he'd expected to. Yet to be perfectly honest, at least with himself, he was reluctant to ponder his feelings for her. "I admit that I enjoy being with her."

Alejandro, who'd yet to celebrate his first wedding anniversary, nodded sagely, as if that's exactly how he'd felt when he started dating Olivia.

Had he enjoyed her company so much that he would have let her rescue two stray mutts, then drive her all around town with them until she found a groomer and a vet? Would he have gladly helped her move into a temporary residence that she'd found on a whim and secured with a lease just as quickly?

Carlo doubted it. And if he listened to his better judgment, he'd realize that Schuyler might prove to be too flighty for him, too prone to change direction with a shift in the wind.

Yet he could just as easily argue against that assumption. Schuyler had found the perfect place in record time. Didn't that imply that she had wisdom, determination and the ability to make things happen?

"So what's holding you back?" Alejandro asked.

From what? "I'm sorry, I'm not following you."

"You might have walked away from the ladies, cousin. But your gaze has been locked on Schuyler for the past five minutes." Alejandro laughed. "Your dad was right. She's got a hold on you. And you've got it bad."

He wanted to object, but it had really begun to feel like that. And that worried him. If he was ever going to consider settling down with a woman, it would have to be one who'd make a lifelong commitment. And Schuyler had made no secret of the fact that she was interested in only fun and games.

But no way would he admit the truth, even to a man he respected to keep his secret. "No, you're wrong. She just amazes me. That's all." Then he changed the subject back to business. "I also had another idea I wanted to run by you."

"What's that?"

"We both have our hands full already, and if we decide to go forward with that nightclub, we'll be busier than ever."

"Actually, if we decide to open that club, you'll be the busy one. It's what you do best. And with that being the case, I'll be here most of the time, doing what I do best."

That was a fair division of labor. And now it was Carlo's turn to nod his agreement.

He took one last look at Schuyler, watched as she told her newfound cousins something that made them all laugh. It would have been nice to have been privy to whatever she'd said. He liked hearing the lilt of her voice, the melodic sound of her laughter.

Unwilling to let Alejandro make any more assumptions, Carlo shook off the distraction and again focused on business. "By the way, Schuyler impressed the hell out of that wedding planner who stopped by the winery a few days ago. The woman thought she was our on-site special event coordinator, and I didn't correct her."

"I see where you're going with this," Alejandro said. "If you think she'd be a good fit for us, I'm okay with it. She's done a great job so far, and I have no reason to doubt her abilities to lock in other weddings and parties. She'd be working with you, though. Do you foresee any future problems?"

Actually, quite a few. But none of them had anything to do with Schuyler's ability to take the ball and run with it.

"No," Carlo said. "I think it'll work out okay."

Now all he had to do was to offer her the position and hope she'd say yes.

"You know," Alejandro added, "if Schuyler wasn't a rock star at representing our brand and so darn good for business, I'd think that you might be trying to strike up points with her for your personal gain."

Carlo stole a glance at his cousin, who was eyeing his pretty bride and probably hadn't realized that his comment had struck a chord.

It was true that Schuyler was a great hostess during those special tastings and a natural-born saleswoman, so it made good business sense to offer her a permanent position with the company, but Carlo's motives were selfish, too. He wanted the opportunity to see her each day.

And there lay his problem. Spending that much time with her was a risky move for a man who didn't make long-term commitments. So he'd better watch out.

The last thing he needed was to get too emotionally involved, especially if his efforts to keep her close for the time being led to a big complication in the future.

Schuyler had always thought La Viña was the perfect place to dine or hold a party. But she'd never guessed that, with a little careful decorating, it would look so festive and romantic. Each linen-draped table had been adorned with white tulle, vases filled with gorgeous red roses and flickering candles.

The string quartet Esteban had hired for the dinner hour had serenaded them all while they dined on oysters in the half shell, a lobster salad on butter leaf lettuce with a citrus vinaigrette, fingerling potatoes and filet mignon with lump crab and hollandaise. As if that wasn't filling, the dessert was to die for: individual chocolate soufflés and long-stemmed strawberries dipped in white chocolate.

Schuyler had attended plenty of other classy parties in the past, each with lovely settings, great music, amazing service and a delicious menu. But none of them had ever energized her quite like this one, which was sure to become a memory she'd never forget.

As the waitstaff began clearing the tables and the disc jockey set up to provide the music for the dance, some of the intriguing people she'd met, as well as a few she'd been observing from a distance, began to mill about the dining room.

Moments ago, after spotting a business associate, Carlo had asked her to excuse him so he could greet the man. Schuyler took the opportunity to get up from the table where they'd been sitting with his father and brothers. She could have continued to chat with his family and gotten to know them even better, but she wanted a chance to not only stretch her legs but to scout the room. So she asked them to excuse her, as well. Then she took a stroll across the room, weaving through the tables until she reached the nearest window that provided a view of the vineyards.

Outside, seated on a wrought iron bench, an older woman with silver-streaked auburn hair seemed to be holding court with several other well-dressed women. She had enough diamond bling around her neck and on her fingers to light up the night sky.

When she turned around, Schuyler realized it was none other than Kate Fortune, the matriarch of the entire Fortune clan. Kate was fiercely devoted to her famous cosmetic company, although she'd recently handed over the CEO reins to Graham Fortune Robinson, a rancher. That move, from what Schuyler had read, had taken the entire family by surprise. But Graham apparently had a business background and just enough out-of-the-box thinking that he impressed Kate. And now that he was in charge, he was doing quite well.

Kate, who was in her nineties, was just as attractive in person as she was in pictures Schuyler had seen. She also appeared to be twenty years younger, thanks to very few facial wrinkles. Her skin had a healthy glow, something that came from having good genes,

Schuyler supposed. Yet it was just as likely a result of the Fortune Youth Serum, which she'd developed and turned into a very successful company that had made her a billionaire.

Schuyler had been intrigued by the stories she'd read about Kate, so to see her in person, even behind a wall of glass, was unbelievably cool.

"Fancy meeting you here," a man said from behind her, his voice laced with the hint of a Texas drawl.

Schuyler turned away from the window to see Nathan Fortune, who'd changed his flannel and denim ranch wear for a stylish suit. "What a surprise." She offered her newfound cousin a friendly smile. "I didn't expect to see you here."

"I make my way to the city every now and then. Besides, I thought Bianca would enjoy a special evening on our first Valentine's Day as husband and wife."

"I'm glad you came. It's nice to see a familiar face."

Nathan scanned the dining room, his eyes taking in the hardwood floors, the wall-to-wall windows, the rounded oak-paneled ceiling. "I heard the restaurant was recently remodeled and expanded. The Mendozas did a great job."

"Yes, they did." Schuyler found it a bit odd that Nathan seemed more interested in the party setting than in the people who'd attended, many of them his relatives. She suspected he was trying to keep his distance and not get too chummy. Hopefully, he wouldn't blow her cover. "I…um…haven't mentioned anything about my…grandfather."

"Don't worry. I won't say anything or reveal your secret. But tell me. I'm curious. What have you found out?"

"Not much. Just that I really like Olivia, Zoe and Rachel, the three cousins I met earlier. But I'm still making my rounds, and the night is young."

"So how are the Mendozas treating you?" Nathan asked. "You must have eased your way into their good graces if you snagged an invitation to the party."

"They've been great." Especially Carlo.

Her gaze drifted across the room, scanning the crowd until she spotted her tall, dark and handsome boss. Her attraction to him continued to grow, which had made her decide to stay in Austin longer than she'd expected to. Maybe, while she was here, she'd be wined and dined—and courted.

Should she invite him back to her place after the party tonight? Or was it too soon? She certainly didn't want to come on too strong. This was one relationship she'd like to last longer than a couple of weeks. In fact, the word *indefinitely* came to mind.

She supposed that was an odd thing for her to ponder, when she'd never thought she'd ever settle down. Not that Carlo would ever want to get married or anything. He'd made it clear how he felt about remaining single. But for some crazy reason, whenever they were together, she found her imagination going off her tried-and-true grid. But that might be due to his kindness to her, his respect for her uniqueness.

"How long do you plan to be in Austin?" Nathan asked, as if reading her mind.

"I'm not sure. I'm actually working for the Mendoza Winery."

"Really? Doing what?"

"I'm a sales rep at special wine tastings. It's only part time, which suits me fine. And, of course, it's just temporary."

"How long is temporary?"

"Who knows? I tend to go with the flow, but I really like it here. The Mendozas are easy to work for."

She'd grouped them all together, even though the one Mendoza she actually answered to was Carlo. But it was true. She liked them all, even Esteban. But it was Carlo who'd caught her eye, touched her heart and held her thoughts.

Sure, he was drop-dead gorgeous. But it was more than sexual attraction that drew her to him. He seemed to accept her and her quirky nature, just as she was. And that didn't happen often.

The two of them had also become a team. Equal partners, it seemed. And her pride, which sometimes faltered when people criticized her, had grown exceptionally strong while working for the winery. She was doing a bang-up job, something all the Mendozas recognized, which gave her a thrill. She wished she could say the same about the feelings her own family evoked.

That, in itself, was enough to make her wonder if it would be in her best interest to consider something more long-term. And she wasn't just considering a professional decision. She was pondering a romantic one, too.

But did she really want to screw up the admiration

she'd achieved and her growing self-respect by letting herself become sexually involved with Carlo?

She glanced across the room again, and her brow furrowed as she spotted him talking to a beautiful brunette who was dressed to the hilt in a flashy red dress and spiked heels. And dang. He was grinning from ear to ear, clearly enjoying their little chat.

When the woman laughed at something he said, Schuyler stiffened. That wasn't good. No, not good at all.

She'd never been the jealous type. Heck, she'd never had reason to be. She'd never cared enough about a man to worry about losing him.

Not that she had any claim on Carlo, but she didn't want to lose him before she even figured out how she felt about him.

Her reason for attending the party in the first place fell by the wayside. All she wanted to do was interrupt that woman's flirtations before… Well, before…

"I'm sorry," she told Nathan. "It's been nice catching up with you, but you'll have to excuse me. There's something I have to do." Something she had to stop.

Before waiting for Nathan's response, she hurried to Carlo's side so she could make her presence—if not her claim on him—known.

Chapter Ten

Carlo had no more greeted Wendy Fortune Mendoza, who'd come all the way from Horseback Hollow with her husband, Marcos, to dance the night away, when Schuyler swept up beside him as if all hell had broken out and the devil was on her trail.

Before he could introduce her to Wendy, his cousin's wife, Schuyler grabbed his hand, gave it a good tug and said, "I need to talk to you."

He had no idea what had her wound up so tight, but he figured it had to be important. And urgent. So he asked Wendy to excuse him, adding, "I'll be back in a moment."

"That's okay," Wendy said. "I was just making the rounds. I'm sure we'll run into each other more than once before the night is over."

Schuyler asked to be excused, too. Then she practically dragged him across the room, her strides causing him to pick up his pace. Something was clearly wrong. Had someone discovered her identity and her reason for being here? Then again, maybe she'd landed a big sales contract for the winery. Or she'd lost one.

Either way, making a mad dash through the restaurant wasn't getting him any answers. He'd at least like a hint. So, as they briskly walked along, he asked, "What's going on?"

Without slowing her steps, she said, "I'll tell you in a minute."

Since they'd just approached a recently vacated table, where no one could overhear their conversation, he pulled back on her hand, making her stop. He studied her intently. "Are you okay?"

She bit down on her bottom lip, and her once-determined expression turned pensive. And a bit flustered.

Before he could suggest that they go outside for some fresh air and privacy, the disc jockey's voice rang out. "Good evening, everyone! What would Valentine's Day be without Elvis Presley singing one of his romantic classics?"

At that, "Fools Rush In" began to play, lulling the crowd and drawing several couples to the dance floor. The familiar tune seemed to work its magic on Schuyler, too.

Her blue eyes widened, sparkling bright. "Oh my gosh, Carlo. I love this song."

The abrupt change in her mood nearly floored him,

but he tamped down his surprise, as well as his confusion. "What did you want to tell me?"

"It can wait for now. Dance with me, Carlo."

He should have balked and demanded an explanation, but he let her lead him to the dance floor. If truth be told, he'd wanted to get his hands on her all night.

So he opened his arms, and she stepped into his embrace. As they swayed to the sensual tune, he savored the feel of her in his arms, the soft feminine curves he would stroke and caress if they didn't have an audience.

Yet several beats later, he felt compelled to ask again. "What was so important that you pulled me away from my cousin's wife?"

Schuyler stiffened, drew back and gazed up at him. A crease marred her pretty forehead. "Your cousin's wife? Is *that* who she was?" She slowly shook her head. "She must think I'm a ditz. And a rude one at that. I'd better apologize to her as soon as this dance is over."

It was beginning to all make sense now. She'd been jealous. He wasn't sure if he should take that as a compliment, laugh or be offended. "Did you think I'd try to hit on another woman when I was with you?"

"Well…you've made no secret about the fact that you're dedicated to the bachelor life."

"Maybe so, but I'd never be disrespectful of the lady I'm with. That's not my style."

"I'm sorry, Carlo. I don't know why I reacted like I did. That's not my style, either."

So he'd been right. Jealousy had provoked her impulsive reaction. He actually took a bit of pride in that and pulled her back into his arms. A wise man might reconsider a relationship with Schuyler, but as he held her in his arms, her head resting against his shoulder, her tantalizing scent doing crazy things to his heartbeat, not to mention his head… Well, hell. He felt like a fool tonight.

In fact, as they continued to dance, he forgot all about business, family and parties. Instead, it seemed as if he and Schuyler were the only people on the dance floor.

Except they weren't. As he steered her through the other couples, he spotted Alejandro and Olivia dancing cheek to cheek, their love for each other apparent.

When Alejandro looked up and caught Carlo's eye, his lips quirked into a crooked grin. *Give love a chance*, he'd told him once. And it seemed that Alejandro was repeating that advice again tonight, only he didn't have to say a single word.

The next couple to ease their way next to him and Schuyler was his father and one of the sales reps, a newly divorced brunette in her early forties. Using some fancy footwork, his wily old man spun his attractive partner to the side, long enough to give Carlo the thumbs-up sign and flash him another atta-boy grin.

Carlo had no more than rolled his eyes at his dad when Chaz and a blonde companion joined them on the dance floor. Carlo would have thought that romance was in the air tonight, that his younger brother had found a lady to woo. But when Chaz let out a slow whistle and gave him the okay sign, Carlo realized that wasn't the case. His family clearly approved of Schuyler, but they were also taunting him, reminding him of all the times he'd sworn to remain single.

Normally he'd be annoyed, but right now he was too caught up in his attraction to Schuyler and his growing arousal.

They danced as if they'd known each other forever— or as if they both planned to get to know each other really well tonight.

What the hell. Whom was he kidding? There was no reason to pretend neither of them knew what was happening.

"I've been thinking," he whispered into her ear. "Maybe we should give a temporary relationship a chance."

She turned her head just enough to catch his eye and smiled. "I'm willing if you are."

Her agreement shot a zing right through him, amping up his desire. "I'd hoped you would say that." He pulled her closer and whispered, "I have to stay until the last guest leaves and the restaurant closes. But if you'll hang out with me, I'll take you home."

Her lips quirked into a sweet but sexy smile. "To your place or mine?"

"Does it matter?"

"Not to me." Then she went up on tiptoes and brushed a kiss on his lips, letting him know they were definitely on the same page. "There's nothing I want more than to be with you tonight."

"Ditto," he said. "It's too bad we have so long to wait."

"I know, but the anticipation will make it all the better."

"And more fun."

"Hey," she said. "Isn't that supposed to be my line?"

"That'll be my motto, too. At least for tonight."

"I have another one," she said. "Life wasn't meant to be boring."

She might be right, but he knew one thing for sure. When it came to being with Schuyler, life would never be dull or routine. But for now, all they had to do was decide where they'd spend the night. So he made the decision for them. "Then my house it is."

The only thing left for them to decide was what they'd have for breakfast.

Schuyler had figured it would be well after midnight till she got to go home with Carlo. But right before the disc jockey announced the last dance, Alejandro had taken Carlo aside and told him to feel free to cut out early.

So they'd left her car at the winery and drove to his place, a luxury apartment in a snazzy high-rise building in downtown Austin.

After he parked in the underground garage, Schuyler walked with him to the elevator. Once inside, they rode it to the fifth floor. Usually, when she was on a date, she'd start having second thoughts long before this. She'd see signs that the man would become possessive and that he'd have unrealistic expectations when it came to her or to their relationship. So she'd find one excuse or another to say good-night and go home alone. She'd found that it was easier to end things rather than risk losing herself or her independence.

She didn't have those same doubts and concerns with Carlo, though. He truly seemed to like her—

unconditionally and just the way she was. He didn't criticize her, and so far, he hadn't made any attempts to change her. And he certainly wouldn't try to tie her down or stake a claim on her. He'd made that pretty clear.

She had to admit that she was a little nervous coming home with him tonight, yet at the same time, she felt a thrill of excitement. The thought of spending the night in his arms and in his bed trumped any butterflies swarming in her stomach.

When they reached his apartment, Carlo unlocked the door and let her inside. The living room was decorated nicely in leather, dark wood and glass. Colorful artwork depicting ocean scenes, sailboats or beach life adorned the walls. But it was the large window that looked out at the city lights that drew her immediate attention.

She walked straight to it and peered into the night. "What an awesome view." She could have stood there indefinitely, admiring the sight, but after all the dancing they'd done this evening, her feet ached. So she kicked off her heels.

The moment she did, she looked over her shoulder at Carlo, then down to her bare feet. "I hope you don't mind if I get cozy."

"Not at all." He removed his suit jacket and placed it on the back of a chair. "Please. Make yourself at home. *Mi casa es su casa.*"

She smiled. "If I was at my house, I'd put on my bunny slippers."

A grin stretched across his face. "Too bad I didn't

buy two pairs. One for you to keep at your place and one to have here."

She liked the sound of that. Apparently, he didn't think one night together would be enough, and she had to agree.

"You never told me," she said, as she turned away from the city view. "How in the world did you find those slippers?"

"I did an internet search for places in Austin that sold funky nightwear. Then I called around till I found them." He loosened his red silk tie, removed it and draped it over his jacket. "Like I said, it was no big deal. Besides, if I would have hit a brick wall, I wouldn't have mentioned anything about them, and you never would have been the wiser."

The fact that he'd put so much thought and effort into finding those slippers pleased her. Carlo was truly one of a kind. A keeper. That is, if he ever wanted to be kept.

"Thanks again," she said. "You scored a lot of points with that gift."

"Oh, yeah?" His eyes twinkled, competing with the stars and the city lights—and winning hands down.

"Yep." In fact, he was racking up points each time she saw him, each time they were together, whether at work or play.

He crossed the room to where she stood. "Can I get you something to drink? Coffee? Water? A nightcap of some kind?"

"No, thanks. I'm not thirsty." Neither was she coy. She knew why she was here. And what she wanted. So did Carlo.

Only trouble was, while he might think otherwise, she wasn't all that experienced sexually. So, rather than making the first move, she'd better let things play out naturally. After all, Carlo had to be a skilled lover. He'd know how to proceed from here, and she'd be in good hands.

But dang. He wasn't making any moves, and she was getting antsy. She'd never been patient when her heart and mind were set on something. And right now, that something was Carlo.

So she stepped forward and slipped her arms around his neck. "I might not be thirsty, but there's something else I'd like."

Apparently, he'd been waiting for her to make the first move because he wrapped his arms around her waist, pulled her flush against him and kissed her as if they'd never stop. Within a heartbeat she was lost in a swirl of heat, passion and desire. An ache settled deep in her core, and Carlo was the only one who could fill it.

She seemed to be stirring up something in him, too. She could feel his blood pounding, his heart beating. Or was that her own?

As their tongues mated, her head spun, and her knees nearly buckled. All she could do was hold on tight and kiss him back.

Their hands stroked, caressed, explored. When he reached her breast, the fabric of her dress bunched up. She had half a notion to stop kissing him long enough to remove the darn thing. Before she could offer the suggestion, his thumb skimmed across her nipple, sending her senses reeling.

About the time she thought she was going to melt into a puddle on the floor, he broke the kiss and said, "Let's take this to the bedroom. I'm not sure how many people are awake at this hour, but with the blinds open and the lights on, we're probably giving them one hell of a show."

She hadn't thought about that. She should have, though. Yet for some reason, it really didn't matter. It wasn't like they were naked. Not yet, anyway.

Carlo took her hand and led her to his king-size bed. If their kisses meant anything at all, making love with him was going to be unimaginable. Amazing. Magical.

Everything about this night felt so good. So right. She was about to tell him that when he caught her jaw in his hand and brought her mouth to his in another earth-spinning kiss that stole her thoughts, her words and, quite possibly, her heart.

Carlo couldn't get enough of Schuyler. As his hands slid along the curve of her back and down the slope of her hips, a surge of desire shot clean through him. He pulled her hips forward, against his erection. She must have realized how badly he wanted her because she whimpered into his mouth and arched forward, rubbing against him, making him grow even harder.

She was driving him crazy, and by the time he thought that the urge to make love would turn him inside out, she tore her mouth away from his, ending the kiss.

Her passion-glazed eyes locked onto his, capturing him and holding him hostage. He ought to run like hell.

Instead, he didn't dare move. In fact, if she had any requests, he'd promise her damn near anything.

She slowly turned around, revealing the back of that alluring red dress. "Unzip me. Please?"

"My pleasure." He did as she requested, then watched as she pushed the fabric over her shoulders and let it drop to the floor.

She stood before him in a skimpy black bra and a matching thong. When she turned to face him, a sexual flush revealed her arousal, her readiness to join him in bed.

Her body, petite yet lithe, was everything he'd imagined it to be and more. He couldn't help marveling at her perfection.

She reached up, removed the clip from her hair, then shook out the thick, glossy strands in a move that was almost his undoing.

While she unhooked her bra, tossed it aside and removed her thong, he unbuttoned his dress shirt and shrugged it off. Once he'd taken off his shoes and the rest of his clothing, he eased toward her, his heart pounding, his blood racing.

She skimmed her nails across his chest, sending a shiver up his spine and a rush of heat through his veins. He couldn't wait any longer. He filled his hands with her breasts, firm and round, the dusky pink tips peaked and begging to be touched, to be loved and kissed.

As he bent and took a nipple in his mouth, she gasped in pleasure. He lavished first one breast, and then the other. All the while, she gripped his shoulder, her nails pressing into his skin.

"I don't know how much more I can take," she said, her words coming out in slow, ragged huffs. "I need to feel you inside me."

Happy to oblige, he lifted her in his arms and placed her on top of the bed. Her luscious blond hair splayed upon the azure blue pillow sham while her perfect body stretched out on the comforter. She lifted her arms toward him, silently urging him to lie with her.

He paused for a beat, drinking in the angelic sight, then he reached into his nightstand drawer and removed several condoms from the box. Something told him they'd need to have plenty of them handy tonight.

With that taken care of, he joined her on the bed, where they continued to kiss, to taste and to arouse each other until they were both eager to become one.

He tore open one of the packets and rolled the condom in place. As he hovered over her, she reached for his erection, opened for him and guided him where he needed to be. The moment he entered her, joining their bodies, a burst of pleasure shot through him. She arched up, meeting each of his thrusts.

This was unbelievable. Staggering, yet in the most surprising sense of the word. He tried to tell himself it was only sex. That it was the same lust that had driven him to propose to Cecily. But nothing he'd ever experienced, ever felt, compared to this. And after tonight, he didn't want to experience it with anyone else.

As Schuyler reached a peak, she cried out and let go. That was all it took to send him over the edge. He shuddered, releasing with her in a sexual explosion that had both his heart and his head spinning.

But as his climax ebbed, realization dawned, and he had to face a startling truth, one that shook him to the core and knocked him for a loop.

He was falling for Schuyler, a woman who claimed to be a romantic tumbleweed, just as he'd once been. And that scared the hell out of him. Schuyler Fortunado had the power to break his heart in two.

They'd both entered this thing—whatever it was— because they thought it might be "fun." But feeling this way about her wasn't fun, and falling in love wasn't a game.

Still, as they lay in the afterglow, Carlo pulled her close, spooning with her in his bed. She seemed to be taking it all in stride. Wasn't she the least bit worried about what was happening? Or did she consider it all fun and games?

He damn sure wouldn't ask. He couldn't face the fact that he'd fallen for a woman who didn't love him back.

For now, he would hold her until the last wave of pleasure subsided, wishing it would never end and knowing it would. Like it or not, it was just a matter of time till Schuyler got a wild hair and moved on to something or someone else.

It was nearly dawn. Schuyler was lying in Carlo's bed, wrapped in the comfort of his arms. Yet it only made her antsy, eager to run away, and she hadn't slept a wink.

She'd spent the last hour reliving each heated touch, each tantalizing kiss. Never in her wildest dreams had she imagined how good their lovemaking would be.

Nor had she realized that she'd end up wanting to spend every night with him. Not just while she was in Austin, but for the rest of her life.

How was that for bad luck?

For as long as she'd been old enough to date, she'd sworn that she didn't want a serious relationship with anyone. And then she'd met Carlo, and she'd begun to reconsider that belief.

At first she'd told herself that her fondness for him was due to the fact that he was fun to be around. And since he felt the same way about commitments that she did, he didn't threaten her independent spirit. But now she realized there was a lot more to it than that. He wasn't the threat. She was.

She'd fallen hard for him, head over heels, heart over brain. And now she had no idea what the morning sun would bring.

He kept a box of condoms handy, within easy reach of his bed. Undoubtedly he had reason to use them often. So what happened if she pushed for something more serious with him, something that might require a commitment from him, if not a ring?

He'd run for the hills. She had no doubt of that. And where would that leave her?

She'd be out of a job, one she really liked and the first she'd ever had that allowed her to shine on her own merits. And worse than that, Carlo's rejection would break her heart.

He lay next to her, his breathing soft and steady, clearly at peace and oblivious to her worries. She glanced at the clock on the bureau. It was nearly five o'clock. If he hadn't brought her here, if she hadn't left her car back at the winery, she would have slipped out of bed quietly and driven home. But she was stuck.

Oh, God. What a mess. And she had only herself to blame. She should have known better.

She rolled to the side. Carlo hadn't yet told her that all good things came to an end, and her heart was already battered and aching. She needed to talk to someone. The only one who'd ever truly understood her was her grandmother, but Glammy was gone. There was one other person she could call. Someone wise and kind. Someone who'd offer her compassion and guidance without judgment.

Of all her brothers and sisters, Everett was the one she looked up to, the one whose judgment was always sound. He was also the one she went to when she was confused or her feelings were hurt.

Everett had made the perfect career choice when he went to medical school. He was a born physician, a healer in every sense of the word. And he'd always been able to put things back to right.

But not this time. She didn't think he could help her straighten out the mess she'd made of her life. Nor could anyone mend her broken heart.

Still, she'd call him the first chance she got. In the meantime, she carefully slipped out of Carlo's embrace, trying her best not to wake him. Then she picked up her discarded clothing and tiptoed to the bathroom.

By the time she'd showered and done her best to

freshen up, the sun had finally risen. And Carlo had woken up.

"Good morning," he said. "You're up early."

"I...um...need to check on the puppies. I called Dottie last night and told her I'd be late coming in and that I'd get them in the morning. But I don't want to take advantage of her, especially when I might need to leave them with her again."

Carlo threw off the covers, revealing his long, lean sexy body in all of his masculine glory. "As soon as I shower, I'll fix a quick breakfast."

Her tummy clenched at the thought of food and after-the-lovin' small talk at the dining room table. But she couldn't surrender to the urge. "That's okay. I'm not hungry. And I rarely eat before nine."

"How about a cup of coffee to go? Or a glass of orange juice?"

She tossed him a breezy smile, hoping he wouldn't see right through it. "I'd better take a rain check."

He nodded. "Sure. No problem. Next time."

Only there wouldn't be a next time. She couldn't allow herself a luxury like that. Not when her emotions were spiraling out of control.

Again, she feigned a smile. "Thanks for a great evening."

"Don't thank me. It was my pleasure." He nodded toward the bathroom. "Give me five minutes, and I'll take you to your car."

True to his word, he was dressed and ready to go within minutes. He hadn't taken the time to shave, which gave him a rough-and-rugged edge, one she found appealing.

On the drive to the winery, neither of them said much. Those fake, carefree smiles had been hard enough to manage. She wouldn't have been able to fake a happy-go-lucky conversation.

Heck, she couldn't even glance across the seat to check out his expression. She was too afraid of what she'd see—and how badly it would hurt.

He pulled into the parking lot and stopped next to her car, but he didn't turn off the engine. No doubt, he was eager to be on his way. Gosh, it hurt just to think about it.

"Thanks again," she said, trying her best to be up-beat. "It was a great party. And last night, at your house, was amazing. We'll have to do it again sometime."

How was that for breezy and carefree?

"You got it." His brow furrowed. "Are you having regrets?"

"About what? Last night?" She waved off the thought with a limp hand. "No, not at all. It's what we both wanted. Right?"

"Yeah."

She lifted her fingers to her lips and blew him a kiss. "I'll talk to you later."

"Yeah."

She grabbed her purse and headed for her car.

Love. Ha! No wonder she'd been so determined to remain single. But even sarcasm didn't take the edge off her ragged feelings.

Carlo didn't drive away. He waited until she got behind the wheel and started her engine. Then he continued to watch until she backed out of the parking space and headed down the driveway.

She'd barely reached the highway when she dialed her brother's number. She usually called him at the office, but not today. He'd still be home.

When he answered, it took her a moment to gather her thoughts and to blink back her tears.

"Hey," she finally said. "What's for breakfast, Doc?" She'd meant her comment to sound normal, as if she wasn't about to burst into tears. But she couldn't squelch a sniffle.

"What's wrong, Schuyler?"

Darn it. He always knew when something was off, even though she rarely cried.

"I...well, I think I've screwed up."

"Didn't I tell you not to chase after the Fortunes?"

"It's not them. I've met quite a few, and all of them have been nice. It's just that..." Her eyes filled with tears, and she tried to blink them back.

"Are you crying?"

She sniffled again. "It's just allergies."

"You don't have allergies."

"I do now. I'm allergic to tall, dark and handsome men."

"Where are you?" he asked.

"I'm in Austin."

"Still? When are you coming home?"

"I don't know. I'm..." Her voice waffled, and her

eyes welled once again. Dang it. She never cried. Well, rarely. She blew out a sigh. "Okay, here's the deal. I've fallen in love with a guy who's determined to remain single the rest of his life."

"You met a man with the same philosophy you have?"

"Yes, that's about the size of it. Only I seem to have changed my mind about weddings and a home in the suburbs with a swing set in the backyard. And it's killing me to feel this way."

"And you've only been in Austin for two weeks? I knew your impulsivity would get you in trouble eventually."

"So it happened fast. But it's real. And it hurts. What should I do, Doc?"

"Pack your things and come home."

"Just like that? I can't. I've got…responsibilities."

"Like what?"

"A job for one thing, although I probably need to quit. It's at the Mendoza Winery, and Carlo—that's the guy I'm dating…well, *was* dating. Anyway, he's the vice president."

"If you don't feel comfortable around him you should leave."

"That's the problem. I've never felt so comfortable around a man in my life. But he's a heartbreak waiting to happen. And it's tearing me up to think about it. I don't want to stay, but I can't leave… I'm so confused."

"Have you talked to him about any of this?"

"Heavens no. I don't want him to flip out. It would

ruin our working relationship. But then again, it's practically ruined already."

"Listen, Schuyler. I'll need to shift some appointments around and change a meeting, but I'm coming to see you in Austin within the next day or so. Hang tight. We'll work through this. And hopefully, by then, you'll be ready to come home."

It was nice to know she had someone in her corner. "Thanks, Doc."

"Where are you staying?"

She gave him the address. "But call first. By the time you get there, I could be at the winery. Or at the dog park."

"Why in the world would you be—" He paused. "Don't tell me you adopted a dog."

"Not one. Two. And they're puppies."

"Do you think that was a good idea?"

"Probably not, but my landlord, who's also my neighbor, has taken a real shine to them. And she looks after them for me sometimes. I guess you could say we're sharing custody at the moment."

When he didn't respond, she said, "Oh, come on, Everett. Don't tell me I'm too irresponsible to be a pet owner, let alone..." She left the rest unsaid.

"I'd never say that, Schuyler. One of these days, when the right man comes along, you're going to be an amazing wife and mom. And you'll get that home in the suburbs."

"You have no idea how much I appreciate your saying that."

"I mean it."

She knew he did. Everett never minced words or tromped on hearts. "I love you, Doc."

"Hang in there. It'll all work out—one way or another."

She wanted to believe him. But something told her that her current problem was one that even Everett couldn't fix.

Chapter Eleven

Twenty minutes after ending her telephone conversation with Everett, Schuyler arrived at her temporary home. She'd told Carlo she needed to check on Fluff and Stuff, and that was on her to-do list. But first she had to get inside her studio apartment before Dottie spotted her wearing the same outfit she'd left in last night.

Not that it mattered. It wasn't anyone's business what she did. At least, that's what she'd always told herself when defending one of her choices in the past.

She'd no more than entered her small digs and kicked off her heels when her phone rang. She assumed Everett had forgotten to tell her something, but when she grabbed her cell and saw Carlo's name on the lighted display, her heart dropped to the pit of her stomach.

As her eyes began to well with tears, she nearly silenced the darn thing. If just seeing his name could set off that kind of visceral response, what would the sound of his voice do to her, let alone the words he might say?

Still, her fingers froze, and the blasted phone continued to ring. If she didn't answer pretty soon, the call would roll over to voice mail before she made the decision to take it or not.

What was wrong with her? She hadn't always made the best choices in the past, but she'd never been indecisive.

Get a grip, Schuyler. What would Glammy do if this were happening to her? She certainly wouldn't put her tail between her legs. She'd take the call.

Schuyler swiped her finger across the screen to answer, just as the ringtone stopped. Great. Now what?

She cleared her throat, shook off her apprehension and returned the call.

When Carlo answered, she let out a nervous little chuckle. "Sorry about that. I couldn't get to my phone in time."

Okay, so that was a lie. And even though it was just a little one, guilt still warmed her cheeks.

"I called to see if you got home okay," Carlo said. "You seemed a little…off when I dropped you at your car. Are you all right?"

Heck no. She was dying inside. And her heart had cracked right down the center. But no way could she reveal that to him. The last thing she wanted was for him to think that she was flaky or weak. That she was a woman who was afraid she couldn't get through life without a man.

"I'm fine," she said.

The conversation stalled for a moment. She tried to rally her thoughts and come up with some kind of feasible script, but it wasn't working.

"You told me you were okay earlier," Carlo said. "But for some reason, I can't buy that."

Probably because she'd told him a lie. A big fat one.

"For the record," he added, "last night was amazing, and I have three empty condom packets to prove it."

He was right about that. Their lovemaking had been everything he said it was. "I couldn't agree more."

"I don't usually make follow-up phone calls," he said. "I never need to. But this is different. I wasn't happy about the way things ended this morning."

She'd take the blame for that. But if she hadn't left when she did, things might have ended a lot worse. She wasn't about to admit that, but she did have to say something. And she couldn't leave him hanging.

"I had a great time at the party," she admitted. "And making love with you was…" A golden memory she'd never, ever forget. "Well, it was awesome. And it could become habit forming."

"And that's a habit you'd rather not have."

Was he expecting confirmation? She could give him that, but it would be yet another lie. She could easily get used to waking in his arms each morning. But they'd agreed to keep things simple.

Hadn't he said he kept his sexual relationships simple?

She'd even assured him that she preferred not to become attached. And then she'd ruined everything by doing an about-face.

"I've always been a little uncomfortable with the after-sex talks," she admitted. And this time it was a whole lot worse.

"Me, too. Those chats can get pretty awkward."

Especially when the two people involved had such different expectations and hopes for the future.

"Don't get me wrong," she added. "Making love was better than good last night. And I really enjoyed it." In fact, way too much. "But can we talk more about this later? I just walked into the house to change my clothes before going to Dottie's to pick up the pups. I'd like to take them for their morning walk before she has to do it."

Now there was an excuse that sounded believable. And it was also consistent with what she'd told him when he dropped her off at her car.

"Sure," he said, "we can talk later. Or we can drop the subject completely. Just keep in mind that I'm the last one in the world who'd ever push you. Or ask more from you than you're willing to give."

Yes, he'd been up-front about that early on. And she'd tried to do the same thing. Then she'd flipped and done a complete one-eighty. And now she was no longer opposed to an exclusive relationship. She was even pondering words like *forever*. And that really should run against her grain. It always had.

"I'm not worried," she lied.

"So you don't have any regrets about last night?"

She had a ton of them, but rather than admit that,

she looked heavenward, hoping she wouldn't get struck by a lightning bolt for her dishonesty. "No, not at all."

"Good. Then there's nothing more to talk about. Let's just take things one day at a time, okay?"

"Sure." She closed her eyes, willing them not to tear up. "It sounds like we're still on the same page."

"By the way," he added, "I scheduled a special tasting at the winery on Saturday afternoon. Are you available to pour at two o'clock?"

Apparently he thought everything was status quo, which meant he wasn't trying to put any distance between them. Of course, he hadn't mentioned anything about that full-time position. But then he probably still had to discuss it with Alejandro.

Still, if that job offer came through, she'd have to turn it down. She couldn't risk being in daily contact with Carlo. Not feeling the way she did.

"I'm free on Saturday afternoon," she told him. "I'll even arrive an hour earlier to make sure everything is set up the way I like it."

"Sounds good. Saturday is also the same night we're going to see *Jersey Boys*. So I'll make sure you're finished in time. Just in case, I'll have Ricardo in the wings as a backup."

With all the emotional upheaval, she'd nearly forgotten their date. The real one she'd been looking forward to.

"I'm not worried about the timing." Her biggest concern was figuring out just how and when to back off.

But then again, wasn't that what she was already doing?

Silence hung on the line.

Finally Carlo said, "I'd better let you go."

That's exactly what she'd been afraid of since early this morning—that he'd make that very decision. And that's why her pride insisted that she let him go first.

Carlo had sensed that Schuyler was withdrawing from him the moment he woke up and saw that she'd already gotten out of bed and showered. In the past, he might have felt relieved that things had gone so smoothly, but that wasn't the case with Schuyler.

He hated to see things end before they even had a chance to get off the ground. Just the thought of her leaving town and going back to Houston nearly choked the breath out of him.

Like it or not, he'd gotten attached.

It's not as if he hadn't seen this coming, either. Ever since he met her, she was all he'd been able to think about. At first, he'd considered her unique and a real novelty. She'd been able to lift his spirits in a special way. She was fun to be with, to laugh with. And for that reason, he'd wanted to spend more and more time with her.

But it was more than that. He'd fallen for her—headfirst and hard. And now that he'd slept with her?

He slowly shook his head at what had become a stark reality. He wanted to stake a claim on a woman who'd made it clear that she was interested only in having fun. And that left him in one hell of a fix.

It also made him feel like a love-struck fool.

He walked across the room, turned and strode back

again, hoping to shake off the compulsion to level with Schuyler, to tell her how he really felt. But how could he do that when she'd obviously sensed it and was pulling away already?

And why wouldn't she? She owned a condo in Houston, where she also had family and had created a life for herself, so she had every reason to return. Hell, even though she was in Austin now, she'd rented that place on a month-to-month lease. She'd moved there from the Monarch Hotel only because of the dogs.

He raked his hand through his hair, then continued to pace his apartment like a caged jungle cat. He needed to talk to someone. Maybe then he could put things in the proper perspective.

Alejandro came to mind, but his cousin was too wrapped up in his new bride and thought everyone else ought to find their own happily-ever-after.

Give love a chance, he'd told Carlo.

Yeah, right. Carlo had tried to do that with Cecily, and where had that gotten him? Hot sex had gone cold within a couple of months. It didn't take a brain surgeon to realize that what he'd thought was love turned out to be lust.

So how could he consider throwing his hat into the marital ring again?

Yet that's the direction his damn thoughts had been leading him. He had to be losing his mind.

Sure, sex with Schuyler had been out of this world— hotter and sweeter than anything he'd ever experienced. But sex wasn't the great equalizer. It took more than that to solve life's problems. He'd learned that lesson when he'd been married to Cecily.

Of course, he'd never smiled as much with her as he did with Schuyler, never enjoyed her company as much. And in the bedroom? There was no comparison.

But Schuyler was sure to blow him off in a few short weeks, if not sooner.

He had to clear his head from fruitless thoughts. He really ought to talk to someone, another bachelor who understood the appeal of great sex, the disappointment of a failed marriage and the need to remain single for life.

The best person would be his father, a man who was the happiest single guy Carlo had ever known. Esteban Mendoza would know just what to say to set things back on track. And the sooner he said it, the better.

Carlo grabbed his cell and made the call. It wasn't until his father answered, his voice sleep-laden, that he realized what time it was.

"I'm sorry," Carlo said. "I didn't mean to wake you."

"That's okay. What's up?"

Carlo blew out a ragged sigh. "I've got a problem, Dad. And I need you to talk me through it."

"Sure, but hang on a minute."

Carlo waited, listening as sheets ruffled, as a groggy feminine voice uttered, "Huh?"

Obviously Carlo and Schuyler weren't the only ones to go home together after a romantic party.

"Shh," his father said. "Go back to sleep, babe. I'll take this call in the other room."

A door clicked shut. Moments later, his father said, "Okay, Carlo, I'm back. What's the problem?"

"I didn't realize you had company. This obviously isn't a good time. We can talk later."

"You rarely call, especially claiming to have a problem. What's going on, *mijo*?"

Carlo raked his hand through his hair, then proceeded to tell his old man what happened and how he was struggling with his feelings.

"I'm not surprised you fell for Schuyler," Esteban said. "I saw it coming before you did."

"You mean when you caught us kissing?"

"No, that's not what clued me in to what was happening. You've kissed plenty of pretty ladies in the past, but I doubt you've ever looked at any of them the way you look at Schuyler. I've seen you smile more in the past couple weeks than in the past ten years. You're happy again, and if you want my opinion, I think you should go for it."

But Carlo *wasn't* happy. He was miserable.

"Thanks for the advice, Dad. But Schuyler isn't interested in having a serious relationship."

"With you?"

"With anyone."

His dad let out a *humph*. "Kind of like you felt before, huh? But you've changed your mind. Maybe, given time, she will, too."

"I doubt that." Carlo slowly shook his head. "And even if she did, I don't want to face another failed relationship. So the only thing I can do is to pull back."

"That won't be easy to do with her working at the winery."

"I'm not sure how long that will last anyway. And so I've been thinking that I'd better not offer her a full-time position. In fact, having her hostess for those special events isn't a good idea, either. Not when she isn't feeling the same thing I am."

"What about that tasting Saturday afternoon?"

"I already asked her to do it, but Ricardo can handle it."

"You'd fire her?"

"If I have to." Wouldn't it be best? Then again, maybe he wouldn't have to go that far. What if he didn't make her working environment so comfortable?

"You could be making a big mistake, *mijo*. Schuyler's done a great job so far."

She'd also done a real number on his heart, and if he didn't figure out a way to send her back to Houston, he'd be toast.

"Yes, I'm sure." He couldn't handle the frustration, either sexual or emotional.

He had to let her go.

"Thanks for letting me talk through this," Carlo said. "Go on back to bed. My head's clear, and I know what to do now."

"Don't do anything rash. You might wind up regretting it in the end."

"I won't." He thanked his dad again, then ended the call.

Once he put away his cell phone, he went into the kitchen and brewed a pot of coffee. He needed a heavy dose of caffeine before setting his plan in motion.

He was going to act cool and unaffected, which years ago had helped him break things off with a woman who'd forgotten their agreement and gotten clingy. If he kept his distance from Schuyler, maybe she'd quit and return to Houston on her own. Either way, he had to end things.

Starting right now.

Everett called Schuyler early on Saturday morning and apologized if he woke her up.

"You didn't. I've already showered, gotten dressed and had breakfast." She didn't blame him for thinking she might still be in bed. She tended to be a night owl, but ever since she'd gone home with Carlo, she hadn't been sleeping very well.

"Where are you?" she asked.

"I just hit the Austin city limits."

"Then you're only ten minutes away from my place. Just meet me here." She'd already given him the address, so she provided him with the easiest directions from the interstate. "I'll see you soon."

While Everett was en route, Schuyler took Fluff and Stuff outside for a potty break. Once her brother arrived, she was going to ask Dottie if she'd dog sit again today.

The front door squeaked open. Schuyler glanced over her shoulder and watched her sweet, pet-loving landlord step out on the porch.

"Good morning," Dottie said. "You're up early."

"My brother is coming to visit."

"That's nice. Will he be staying with you? Not that it matters. I'm just curious."

"I'm not sure." If Everett had his way, Schuyler would be following him home tonight.

And maybe that wasn't such a bad idea after all.

"How long will he be visiting?"

"Just a day or so. I thought I'd take him around Austin and show him the sights."

"I'd be happy to watch Fluff and Stuff—unless you're going to take them with you."

"You don't mind?"

"I'd love to. I'm growing very fond of these sweet little rascals."

"That would be great. Thanks, Dottie."

The women and the dogs were still in the front yard when Everett arrived.

"Hey," Schuyler called out as he got out of his car. "You found me."

"It wasn't hard."

Gosh, it was good to see him in person. Not that he'd provide an instant cure for her heartbreak, but having him here would help.

Schuyler introduced him to Dottie. "Everett is a doctor in Houston."

Dottie reached out to shake his hand. "How nice to have a physician in the family."

Yes, that was true. But there was more to Everett than his medical degree. He was one of the smartest men Schuyler had ever met. He did get a little hyper-focused at times, but only because he was determined to be the best doctor in the world. He also had a kind and sympathetic heart.

Schuyler was actually surprised he hadn't gotten married yet. She would have thought some woman would have snatched him up by now.

He was attractive, too. At six feet tall, he was both lean and buff. With his dark hair and expressive blue eyes, he reminded her of a young Christian Bale. Not so much today, though. He was wearing glasses, which he sometimes did.

Schuyler liked seeing them on him. They made him look even extra bright and not the least bit geeky.

"Well," Dottie said, stooping to pick up Stuff, who'd jumped up on her leg, "it was nice to meet you, Doctor. If you'll excuse me, I'll take these little rascals inside and leave you two to visit and take that drive. Maybe you'll see why Austin is so appealing."

"Thanks, Dottie. And don't worry, I'll show him all the sights." Then she turned to her brother. "Have you had breakfast yet?"

"Yes, before I left Houston. I'm not hungry now, but I'll probably want an early lunch."

"That works for me."

Everett scanned the yard, taking in Dottie's two-story brick house, the tree-lined street and the quiet neighborhood.

"What do you think of my temporary digs?" she asked.

"It seems like a nice place to live, but this isn't anything like your loft condo in downtown Houston. And it seems a little too much like suburbia to suit you for very long."

He might be right, but she'd found it peaceful.

"Have you given any thought to coming home with me?" he asked.

"Yes, but I have some commitments. I have a wine tasting to hostess this afternoon." She also had a date tonight, but she was going to cancel that, using her brother's "surprise" visit as her excuse. She couldn't have made up a better one than that.

"So where are the sights you're going to show me?" Everett asked.

The only one that came to mind was the winery. So why not take him there? After all, that's what had kept her in Austin. Well, that and the handsome Latino vice president who didn't love her back.

As much as she'd like to avoid Carlo, maybe it would be best if she did find him there. That way, Everett would understand why she was so taken by him and why she was so confused about what to do.

"You know," Schuyler said, "let's drive out to the Mendoza Winery. I think you'll like seeing it, and it'll also give me a chance to introduce you to my new friends."

"That's fine with me. Do you want to take my car or yours?"

"I'll drive."

Twenty minutes later, they arrived at the winery and parked near several familiar cars, including Carlo's. Her heart made a swan dive, then belly flopped. Had she made a bad decision to face him?

"This is impressive," Everett said, as he unbuckled his seat belt.

Well, there really was no getting around it now. Worst-case scenario, upon seeing Carlo she'd break into tears. And if that happened, she'd drive home, pack up her things and her dogs and follow her brother back to Houston.

It wasn't the greatest game plan, but it was the best she had. "Come on, Doc. I'll show you around."

She pointed out the tasting room, as well as La Viña, then led him to the winery office. She opened the door and found Esteban and Alejandro bent over a desk and going over an order.

Esteban straightened. He glanced first at Schuyler, then focused his gaze on Everett. He wasn't wearing his usual smile, which was odd, but she'd probably interrupted a business conversation.

Schuyler introduced the men to Everett, mentioning the title he'd earned and explaining he was her brother. At that, Esteban seemed to forget business matters and smiled.

"Where's Carlo?" she asked.

Esteban was the first to answer. "He and his brothers took the truck and went to the distribution center at Austin Commons."

The fact that Carlo wasn't around was both reassuring and disappointing. She realized that was why a relationship with him wouldn't be in her best interests. Her feelings for him were too complicated, too confusing.

"Doctor, how long will you be in town?" Alejandro asked.

"Just a day or so. I'm trying to talk Schuyler into going back to Houston with me."

Esteban arched a brow. "Is it working?"

Tears welled in her eyes, and she blinked them back. "I never expected to remain in Austin very long."

"Then I guess that means you won't be interested in taking on a full-time position here," Alejandro said. "I'm sorry to see you go, but if you ever decide to relocate to Austin, you have a job here."

A single tear overflowed, and she swiped it away, hoping no one had seen it. She had to clear her throat before she could trust herself to speak. "Thanks, Alejandro. Anyway, I guess I'll be back around one o'clock this afternoon for that wine tasting."

She glanced at her brother, then nodded at the door, signaling she was ready to leave. She'd held it together the best she could, but if they didn't go now, she'd fall completely apart.

After a quick tour of Austin, which didn't take very long since Schuyler was pretty much a tourist herself, she and Everett stopped at a trendy sandwich shop not far from Austin Commons. They ordered lunch at the counter, then found a quiet table nearby and waited until a teenage server brought them their food.

When the young man had gone back behind the counter, she picked up her fork, then said, "I'd like for you to go with me to that tasting at the winery this afternoon. Regardless of how things turned out for me here, I love their wine. And I know you will, too. I dare you not to order a case or two to take home with you."

"With *us*, right?"

Reluctantly, she agreed. It was for the best.

Everett bit into his sandwich, and Schuyler had no more than taken a forkful of her salad when the door of the eatery opened and two women walked in. Schuyler didn't give them a second glance, but Everett did.

He straightened, then set down his sandwich.

"What's the matter?"

He didn't answer right away. Instead, he watched the women order a couple of brownies to go.

"Do you know them?" she asked.

"The redhead is Lila Clark."

Schuyler put down her fork and studied her brother's rather perplexing expression. "Who's she?"

"A girl I dated in high school." He continued to study her, as if the surprise sighting had thrown him for a loop.

Schuyler could see why. There was a quiet beauty about Lila. And her long straight auburn hair was striking. She wore a floral-printed skirt and a matching pale green blouse. She also had on a pair of ballet flats, which made Schuyler wonder if she was a little self-conscious about her height. Not that she was *that* tall.

"I was just a kid when you were in high school," Schuyler said, "but I never knew you dated anyone. You always had your nose in a book."

Apparently, he'd set those books down once in a while.

"What's she doing in Austin?" Schuyler asked.

"I have no idea. I haven't seen her in more than a decade."

"You should go say hello."

Everett slowly shook his head. "No, that's not a good idea. We've both moved on, created different lives."

Maybe so, but he continued to watch Lila, his eyes pained. Did she dare ask what had gone wrong? Why they'd split up?

"Lila looks good," he said. "But her eyes aren't as bright as I remember."

"Maybe she's having a bad day."

"Maybe." Everett studied her a bit longer. "But there's something sad about her."

Schuyler had no way of knowing. And she wasn't sure what to say.

Oddly enough, after Lila and her friend left with their brownies in a small bag, Everett stopped talking to her about leaving Austin. Instead, he looked up, his gaze locked on hers. "If you love Carlo, you should fight for him—the way I should have fought for Lila."

If Schuyler hadn't been so wrapped up in her own hurts, she might have quizzed her brother more about his broken teenage romance.

Instead, she pondered his advice. *Fight for Carlo.*

Schuyler had never needed to fight for anything. But then again, she'd never wanted anything that badly.

Meeting the Fortunes had come close, which was why she was here.

Carlo was definitely worth fighting for—if she could guarantee a win.

What would Glammy do?

Maybe there was a better question. What was Schuyler going to do?

Chapter Twelve

Everett remained quiet and pensive on the drive to the winery. Schuyler suspected he was reflecting on Lila and his high school days. Then again, he could just as easily be pondering a medical issue facing one of his patients back home.

She might have asked him to share his thoughts with her, but she was too busy trying to figure out what she was going to say to Carlo when she got him alone.

When Everett suggested that she "fight" for him, she'd agreed. But she wasn't sure how to go about that. It wasn't like she could actually do anything to change his mind or convince him to give up his bachelor life-style and settle down with one woman, namely her.

Maybe she should start out by laying it on the line. She could tell him how she felt, then apologize for not sticking to the agreement they had to keep things light and simple. At that point, the ball would be in his court.

She stole another glance at her brother, who was gazing out the passenger window, watching the landscape pass by. She was tempted to draw him out of his musing so she could practice what she was going to say to Carlo, but that was one speech she'd have to come up with on her own.

When they arrived at the winery, she didn't see Carlo's car, which was a little surprising. Was he trying to avoid her? Her chest tightened at the thought, squeezing her heart, which was already crushed.

Well, she'd just have to wait until he returned. Then she'd face him and whatever resulted from her confession, whether that was tears or hugs and kisses.

But hey. Life wasn't meant to be boring—or predictable. Right?

Rather than take Everett with her to the tasting room, she stopped by the office first. That way, she could ask someone where Carlo went and when he'd be back.

That someone was Alejandro, who sat at his desk. When Schuyler and Everett entered, he looked up from his work and smiled.

"Is Carlo around?" she asked, even though she knew he wasn't.

"He *was* here." Alejandro set his pen aside. "But he left when Esteban told him you were planning to leave town."

What was that supposed to mean? Was Alejandro suggesting that Carlo had reacted negatively to the news? That he might actually feel more for her than he'd admitted to? That he was saddened to hear she was going back to Houston?

Maybe she'd read him wrong.

"I get the sense that you care for him," Alejandro said.

"You're right. I didn't want it to happen, and neither did he. But I fell in love with him." She bit down on her bottom lip, then looked to Alejandro, hoping he had some answers for her. "Did he say anything about me? About us?"

"No, he was pretty tight-lipped. But don't follow his lead. You two really need to talk it out."

Alejandro was right. She glanced at Everett, who was nodding in agreement.

"All right," she said. "Where did he go?"

"Home. He lined up Ricardo to pour at the tasting this afternoon and then gave him a list of things to do for him while he was gone. He said he needed to get away for a while."

That didn't sound good. Something was definitely wrong. And a phone call wasn't going to fix it.

She turned to Everett. "I need to talk to him alone."

"You're right."

And that meant she had to leave Everett here. "Alejandro, do you mind entertaining my brother while I'm gone?"

"No, not at all."

"Maybe you could let him have a taste of the Red River. Everett has always been partial to merlot." Then she hurried out the door, reaching into her purse for her keys before getting anywhere near her car.

* * *

Carlo had never felt such a strong compulsion to escape, to get his head together. Schuyler was leaving. And not some day in the near future. Apparently she was going *now*.

When his father had told him that she'd made plans to return to Houston, the axis that held his world together had shifted, leaving him stunned.

"Her brother was with her," his father had added. "He's a doctor and seems like a nice guy."

The good doctor must have influenced her decision to go, although Carlo wasn't entirely sure anyone could actually persuade Schuyler to do anything. But that didn't really matter.

She was going. He was hurting. And he'd be damned if he wanted anyone to know that she'd had that big of an effect on him.

That meant he couldn't hang around the winery, where someone was bound to pick up on his mood. And he couldn't very well slip off without letting his cousin know what he had in mind. So he'd gone in search of Alejandro and found him in the office.

"Listen," Carlo had said, "I'm going to need to take some time off."

"Sure. It's not like you haven't earned it. When?"

"Now. I'll fill in Ricardo on the things he'll need to do to cover for me, then I'm going home to pack."

Alejandro studied him for a moment, as if he could see right through him. "Does this have anything to do with Schuyler leaving town?"

Carlo'd slowly shook his head. "No, it's a coincidence. I just need some time away."

"Will a week be enough?"

Maybe. Hopefully. "Yes," he'd said.

"Where are you going?"

"I'm not sure." The place would have to be warm and tropical, somewhere he could find a beach and let the ocean lull him and allow him to heal. "The Bahamas maybe. Possibly Belize or Cancún. I'll figure it out on my way home."

Damn. When had he ever taken off on a whim to parts unknown? He was behaving as impulsively as Schuyler. Still, it seemed to be the only thing he could do right now.

"Are you going to talk to Schuyler before you go?" Alejandro had asked.

"No, that's not necessary." It's not like Carlo would be able to change her mind about leaving. Besides, she had her life to live, and he had his.

"Do you want to talk about this?" his cousin had asked.

"No, there really isn't anything to talk about." And certainly not with a happily married guy who'd probably forgotten what it was like to be single and carefree.

Alejandro wouldn't understand what it felt like to have his life upended by a beautiful bohemian, to have his heart broken and then to have to figure out a way to pick up the pieces before anyone realized his vulnerability and his pain.

After thanking his cousin for understanding his need to get away, as well as his desire to keep his thoughts to himself, he went home to retrieve a few things he'd need on his upcoming trip—boxer briefs, casual shorts and T-shirts, a couple of swim trunks.

As he stacked them on top of the dresser, he couldn't help noticing the tickets he'd purchased for tonight's performance of *Jersey Boys*. He wouldn't be using them now. Should he give them away?

Maybe Schuyler would like to take her brother. Then again, that would require him to talk to her, to meet with her so he could give her the tickets.

He'd just pulled his suitcase from the closet when his doorbell rang. He rarely got uninvited guests, so he couldn't imagine who it could be.

He left his suitcase on the bed and went to open the door. His breath caught when he spotted Schuyler. She was dressed in that killer black dress she wore when she was a hostess for some of the wine tastings.

She offered him a shy smile, and his knees nearly buckled, weakening him even further. It wasn't a good feeling.

He meant to act cordial, unaffected by her presence. But his tone came out a little harsh when he asked, "What are you doing here?" He didn't apologize for it, though. Her arrival had taken him by surprise, and he was too broken up, too scattered to be polite.

She tucked a strand of hair behind her ear. "I came by to…check on you."

"Why? I'm fine."

"Alejandro said you were taking some time off."

He nodded. "Yeah. I've got some things to do that I've been putting off."

"Does this have anything to do with me? With…us?"

Of course it did. Any fool could see that. Hell, Alejandro had figured it out, even if Carlo had refused to admit it. Surely Schuyler had, too. Wasn't that why she was here? To tell him she was sorry that he'd let himself get in too deep? To explain why it was best for both of them if she left town? If it weren't so freaking sad and painful, he'd laugh.

"No, Schuyler, my vacation doesn't have anything to do with you."

"Are you sure?"

At that, he almost laughed. If he told her the truth, she'd take off at a dead run back to Houston faster than a speeding bullet.

Don't show any emotion. Think about your pride. You can do this.

"I'm sure." The polite thing to do was to invite her inside, but he couldn't do that.

"When are you leaving?" she asked.

"As soon as I finish packing." He thought of the suitcase on the bed, the clothes he'd stacked next to those tickets.

Realizing they'd go to waste—and that she was already here—he said, "I'm not going to be able to see that show tonight, but I'll give you the tickets. Your brother may enjoy seeing it."

Her eye twitched, then she slowly shook her head. "No, we'll be on the road to Houston by then. You'd better give them to someone else."

"Okay. Drive carefully. If I don't see you again, I hope you find everything you're looking for."

"Thanks. You, too." She nodded toward the hall elevator. "I'd better go. My brother is back at the winery, waiting for me."

He was tempted to tell her to keep in touch. But it was hard enough watching her go now. He'd be damned if he wanted to put himself through the pain again.

As the door clicked shut, he pondered his next move while regretting he had to make this one.

By the time Schuyler reached her car, hot tears were streaming down her face. She'd no more than swipe them away, when they'd spill over again.

She'd been wrong. Carlo didn't feel anything special for her.

You two need to talk, Alejandro had said.

Yeah, right. And just look where that stupid advice had gotten her. Her heart ached more than ever, and her pride had all but been crushed.

On the upside, he'd offered to give her the two tickets to *Jersey Boys*. She rolled her eyes at the absurd gesture. There was no way she'd be able to go out this evening and enjoy the show. As it was, she'd have to avoid her favorite oldies radio station so she wouldn't hear a song by the Four Seasons and remember the man she lost.

When she reached the winery and parked, she glanced at her image in the rearview mirror. Her eyes were so red and puffy, she'd never be able to hide the fact that she was heartbroken.

Everyone would know, and then they'd tell Carlo.

But so what? At this point, nothing seemed to matter anymore.

She got out of the car, slammed the door and made her way into the winery office, where her brother was sipping on red wine. A fancy white cardboard box bearing the Mendoza label rested next to him.

So she'd been right. He did like that merlot enough to purchase a case to take home.

When Everett looked at her face and realized she'd been crying, he got to his feet, set his wineglass aside and gave her a hug. "I'm sorry, Schuyler. I take it things didn't go very well."

"Good guess." She pulled free of his brotherly embrace and gestured toward the door. "Come on. Let's go. I need to get out of here. If we get on the road within an hour, we'll be back in Houston before dark."

All she had to do was pack. It wouldn't take long to get her things together, but she'd need to get the dogs' stuff, too. She'd also have to tell Dottie she was leaving.

She had a feeling that Dottie would offer to keep Fluff and Stuff, but Schuyler couldn't leave them behind. Having the dogs to care for might help ease her pain, if that was even possible. But at least she wouldn't be entirely alone.

Since Dottie was on a limited income, Schuyler would offer to pay her several months' rent. It was only fair. And it would tide the kindhearted woman over until she found another tenant.

Everett had no more than picked up the case of wine, when Esteban entered the office.

"Before you leave," Carlo's father said, "I'd like to have a word with you."

She couldn't imagine what he had to say to her, but

he'd always been kind. She couldn't refuse him. "All right."

Esteban made an after-you gesture with his hand, pointing to the door. "Let's go outside where we can talk privately."

She agreed, and they stepped out into the yard.

"I heard that you were leaving today," he said.

"Yes, I'm going back to Houston."

"That seems like a pretty sudden decision."

"Not really. But I've always been a little impulsive."

He nodded, as if giving that some thought. "Did you know that Carlo is leaving, too?"

"Yes, he told me."

"My son has never been impulsive."

Schuyler's eyes filled again. "Maybe not, but I think he's trying to distance himself from me."

"That's probably true. But your red, swollen eyes suggest you're not happy about that."

She blew out a sigh. "I guess it's not a big secret. We started flirting with each other, and we both were determined to keep things simple. But then I went and ruined it all by falling in love with him."

"Have you told him?"

"I was going to, but he wasn't at all happy to see me and practically threw me out of his apartment."

"He told you to leave?"

"No, but he was pretty cold. He told me to have a good life."

Esteban reached out and placed a fatherly hand on her shoulder. "Carlo didn't mean to hurt you, *mija*."

Schuyler rolled her eyes. "So you say. But you

weren't standing in his doorway, wondering if he'd invite you inside and realizing that he couldn't send you away fast enough."

"All of my boys are headstrong and love-shy. After growing up in a house with two unhappy parents who fought more often than not, they've all pretty much vowed to be single. Especially Carlo, who gave marriage a try, only to see it end within a year."

"Yes, I know about that. He told me."

"But what he didn't tell you is that, in spite of himself, he loves you."

"That's not the vibe I got twenty minutes ago."

"That's because Carlo's afraid to tell you how he really feels."

She wanted to believe that, but she couldn't risk finding out that Esteban was wrong. That if Carlo had any feelings for her, they weren't strong enough to last. "I'm sorry, but I'm not going to face him again. Not after the words he said and the tone he used today."

Still, she didn't rush back into the office and tell Everett her chat with Carlo's father was over, that she was ready to go now.

"Carlo has my number," she finally said. "If he changes his mind, he can call me in Houston."

Before Esteban could respond, she heard a car engine. Schuyler suspected the people who were coming to this afternoon's tasting had begun to arrive. But when she glanced into the parking lot, she spotted Carlo.

She watched as he strode forward, clearly approaching her. But this time, when they were face-to-face, she was the one to ask, "What are you doing here?" And not very nicely.

"I came to apologize."

"For what?" she asked, not about to make it easy on him. "For being a jerk?"

He nodded. "After the party, we got off on the wrong foot. And things got progressively worse."

"Actually, it wasn't until I woke up in your bed that things went downhill."

Esteban folded his arms across his chest and looked at Carlo sternly. "Since you refused to admit it, I told Schuyler how you really feel about her."

Schuyler studied Carlo, wondering if what his father had said was true. If so, would Carlo actually admit it?

Carlo wasn't happy that his father interfered with his love life, but his dad was right. And just looking at Schuyler's splotchy, tear-stained face told him that she might care more for him than she'd let on.

"I do love you," he told her. "I know it's not what either of us planned. But I couldn't help it. And I was afraid to tell you because I thought you'd retreat and move back to Houston."

"Seriously?"

There was no point denying it now. Thanks to his dad, the romantic cat was out of the bag. "You're all I think about, Schuyler, and once I realized all I stood to lose…well, I started to withdraw."

"But you're here," she said.

"After you left, I realized that I'd just shot myself in

the foot. So I figured I'd better try to make things right. I'll do whatever I can to convince you to stay."

"Okay," she said.

"Okay, as in you'll give me a chance to prove myself and make things better between us?"

"No," she said, shaking her head while a smile danced on her lips. "Okay as in I'll stay. I'm not leaving. And if you would have given me a minute to explain, I would have told you that I love you, too. It's clear to me that we belong together."

Any apprehension, any fears Carlo once had, dissipated in the air, replaced by hope. "You've got that right, honey."

Esteban, who'd been eavesdropping and clearly enjoying it way too much, laughed. "Then what are you waiting for, *mijo*? Don't let me stop you. Go ahead and kiss her!"

Carlo couldn't think of anything he'd like to do more—other than taking her home with him and making love until dawn. But that could wait.

For now, he wrapped his arms around Schuyler and kissed her with all the love in his heart, all the hope he had for a future together. By the time they came up for air, Alejandro and a guy who had to be Schuyler's brother had joined them outside.

"I believe I hear wedding bells," Esteban said.

"I hope you do," Carlo told his father. "Because I'm going to propose as soon as I buy a ring. And hopefully, she'll say yes."

Schuyler laughed. "I don't need a ring. So if you're proposing—and I have witnesses—I'll tell you right now my answer is yes." Then she threw her arms around his neck and kissed him soundly and with assurance that she'd heard those bells, too.

This time, when the kiss ended, Schuyler was crying.

"What's the matter?" he asked. "You're not having second thoughts, are you? Was a proposal too much, too soon?"

"My mind is set, Carlo. These are happy tears. I can't wait to be your bride."

Carlo turned to his cousin. "I still plan to take some time off, but now Schuyler will be with me. Can you get by without us for the next week or so?"

"Are you going someplace?" Alejandro asked.

"We'll see how we feel after all the fairy dust settles, but I'd be content to hole up at my place."

Schuyler laughed. "That sounds like an amazing plan to me."

Esteban elbowed Alejandro. "Well, what do you know? The two people who never wanted to tie the knot realize they can't live without each other."

That was the truth.

"Schuyler," her brother said. "Aren't you going to introduce me to your future husband?"

"Oh my gosh. I'm so sorry." She turned to Carlo. "This is my brother, Dr. Everett Fortunado."

The good doctor reached out his hand, but Carlo embraced him instead. "It's nice to meet you, Doctor."

"Call me Everett. And the pleasure is all mine. I'm glad to see my little sister so happy." He turned to Esteban and Alejandro. "It was nice meeting you both. I'm sure we'll see each other again soon."

Esteban wore a proud, father-of-the-groom grin. "No doubt at the wedding, if not sooner."

Everett reached out his hand to Schuyler. "Let me have your car keys."

"Where are you going?" she asked.

"It looks like you have another ride, so I thought I'd take your car back to your place, exchange it for mine and hit the road."

Schuyler went inside for her purse, then handed the keys to her brother. "Thanks for coming."

"You're more than welcome. I'll see you soon." Then he turned and walked away.

Carlo glanced at his watch. "You know, since we both have some time off, why don't we go to my apartment. I still have those tickets to *Jersey Boys.*"

"That sounds like a great idea. We can go…if we don't get sidetracked."

Carlo liked the sound of that. "Let's see how the afternoon unfolds." Then he took Schuyler's hand and led her to his car.

"I can't wait to see what life has in store for us," she said.

Neither could he. But right now, he was looking forward to spending the afternoon in bed with her.

The sun had just begun to set, darkening the bedroom, as Carlo and Schuyler snuggled in bed, enjoying the afterglow of another heart-stirring, star-spinning climax.

"We can still make the show," he said, as he rolled

to the side, bracing himself with his elbow. "That is, if you want to go."

"I'd like that, if you don't mind." Still, neither of them moved.

"I was thinking," he said. "Maybe we should find another place to live. Since I'm going to marry you, that'll make me a dog owner. So we'll need a house, one that's pet friendly and has a big, fenced yard."

"That's sweet of you. Just so you know, I talked to Dottie earlier, and she agreed to keep the puppies for a while. I have a feeling it'll be hard for her to give them up. We might have to take one and let her keep the other."

Carlo laughed. "Let's take Fluff. She won't be as expensive to feed. Stuff eats a ton."

"Good idea." Schuyler brightened, then rolled to her side, facing him. And loving the sight of him, naked and stretched out beside her.

"I have a question for you," he said, as he trailed his fingers along the slope of her hip. "What do you plan to do about the Fortunes? You've met quite a few, and you've told me you liked them. Are you going to announce that you're related to them?"

"Maybe, but not right away." She brushed a fallen hank of hair from his brow and smiled. "Now that I'm going to be a Mendoza, there's no rush. I have a feeling there'll be plenty of Fortunes in my future."

And if Carlo had anything to say about it, there'd be some little Mendozas in her future, too.

* * * * *

Don't miss the next installment of the new
Harlequin Special Edition continuity
THE FORTUNES OF TEXAS:
THE RULEBREAKERS.

After high school, Everett Fortunado could never
find a woman who measured up to his first love,
Lila Clark. But when they meet again, they find that
putting the past behind might not be so easy...

Look for
THE FORTUNE MOST LIKELY TO...
by USA TODAY *Bestselling Author*
Marie Ferrarella.
On sale March 2018,
wherever Harlequin books and ebooks are sold.
And catch up with the Fortune family by reading
HER SOLDIER OF FORTUNE
by Michelle Major.

Available now!

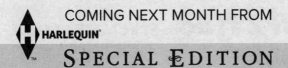

COMING NEXT MONTH FROM

HARLEQUIN®

SPECIAL EDITION

Available February 20, 2018

#2605 THE FORTUNE MOST LIKELY TO...
The Fortunes of Texas: The Rulebreakers • by Marie Ferrarella
Everett Fortunado has never quite gotten over his high school love, Lila Clark. So when circumstance offers him a second chance, he grabs it. But is Lila willing to forget their past and risk her heart on a millionaire doctor with ties to the Fortunes?

#2606 THE SHERIFF'S NINE-MONTH SURPRISE
Match Made in Haven • by Brenda Harlen
After a weekend of shared passion, Katelyn Gilmore doesn't expect to see Reid Davidson again—until she meets Haven's new sheriff! But she has a surprise, too—scheduled to arrive in nine months...

#2607 A PROPOSAL FOR THE OFFICER
American Heroes • by Christy Jeffries
Fighter pilot Molly Markham is used to navigating her own course. Billionaire Kaleb Chatterson has never found a problem he couldn't fix. But when the two pretend to be in a fake relationship to throw off their families, neither one has control over their own hearts.

#2608 THE BEST MAN TAKES A BRIDE
Hillcrest House • by Stacy Connelly
Best man Jamison Porter doesn't believe in a love of a lifetime. But will his daughter's adoration of sweet—and sexy—wedding planner Rory McClaren change this cynical lawyer's mind about finding a new happily-ever-after?

#2609 FOREVER A FATHER
The Delaneys of Sandpiper Beach • by Lynne Marshall
After a devastating loss, Daniel Delaney just wants to be left alone with his grief and his work. But his new employee, the lovely Keela O'Mara, and her daughter might be just the people to help remind him that love—and family—can make life worth living again.

#2610 FROM EXES TO EXPECTING
Sutter Creek, Montana • by Laurel Greer
When Tavish Fitzgerald, a globe-trotting photojournalist, gets stuck in Montana for a family wedding, one last night with Lauren Dawson, his hometown doctor ex-wife, leads them from exes to expecting—and finally tempts him to stay put!

YOU CAN FIND MORE INFORMATION ON UPCOMING HARLEQUIN® TITLES, FREE EXCERPTS AND MORE AT WWW.HARLEQUIN.COM.

HSECNM0218

Get 2 Free Books,
Plus 2 Free Gifts—
just for trying the Reader Service!

*Everett Fortunado never got over his high school love,
Lila Clark. So when circumstance offers him a second
chance, he grabs it with both hands. But is Lila willing
to forget their past and risk her heart on a millionaire
doctor with ties to the Fortunes?*

Read on for a sneak preview of
THE FORTUNE MOST LIKELY TO...
by USA TODAY *bestselling author*
Marie Ferrarella, *the next installment in*
THE FORTUNES OF TEXAS:
THE RULEBREAKERS *continuity.*

Before Lila could ask any more questions, she suddenly
found herself looking up at Everett. The fund-raiser was
a black-tie affair and Everett was wearing the obligatory
tuxedo.

It was at that moment that Lila realized Everett in a tuxedo
was even more irresistible than Everett wearing scrubs.

Face it, the man would be irresistible even wearing a kilt.

"What are you doing here?" Lila asked when she finally
located her tongue and remembered how to use it.

"You know, we're going to have to work on getting you
a new opening line to say every time you see me," Everett
told her with a laugh. "But to answer your question, I was
invited."

Lucie stepped up with a slightly more detailed explanation
to her friend's question. "The invitation was the foundation's
way of saying thank you to Everett for his volunteer work."

"Disappointed to see me?" he asked Lila. There was a touch of humor in his voice, although he wasn't quite sure just what to make of the stunned expression on Lila's face.

"No, of course not," Lila denied quickly. "I'm just surprised, that's all. I thought you were still back in Houston."

"I was," Everett confirmed. "The invitation was express mailed to me yesterday. I thought it would be rude to ignore it, so here I am," he told her simply, as if all he had to do was teleport himself from one location to another instead of drive over one hundred and seventy miles.

"Here you are," Lila echoed.

Everything inside her was smiling and she knew that was a dangerous thing. Because when she was in that sort of frame of mind, she tended not to be careful. And that was when mistakes were made.

Mistakes with consequences.

She was going to have to be on her guard, Lila silently warned herself. And it wasn't going to be easy being vigilant, not when Everett looked absolutely bone-meltingly gorgeous the way he did.

As if his dark looks weren't already enough, Lila thought, the tuxedo made Everett look particularly dashing.

You're not eighteen anymore, remember? Lila reminded herself. *You're a woman. A woman who has to be very, very careful.*

She just hoped she could remember that.

Don't miss
THE FORTUNE MOST LIKELY TO…
by Marie Ferrarella, available March 2018 wherever
Harlequin® Special Edition books and ebooks are sold.

www.Harlequin.com

LOVE
Harlequin
romance?

Join our Harlequin community to share your thoughts and connect with other romance readers!

Be the first to find out about promotions, news, and exclusive content!

Sign up for the Harlequin e-newsletter and download a free book from any series at **www.TryHarlequin.com**

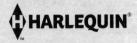

THE WORLD IS BETTER WITH
Romance

Harlequin has everything from contemporary, passionate and heartwarming to suspenseful and inspirational stories.

Whatever your mood, we have a romance just for you!

Connect with us to find your next great read, special offers and more.

f /HarlequinBooks

🐦 @HarlequinBooks

www.HarlequinBlog.com

www.Harlequin.com/Newsletters

H HARLEQUIN®

A *Romance* FOR EVERY MOOD™

www.Harlequin.com